BOUND BY THE GODDESS

THE MORRIGAN SOUL BOND SERIES

SELINA BEVAN

Cover Design by: Leigh Cover Design

Editing by Dayna Hart

ISBN: 978-1-916719-02-6

CONTENT NOTES

This is a Why Choose romance which means there are steamy scenes between one woman and three men. There are no swords crossing. There are, however, tentacles. Lots and lots of tentacles.

Also in this book: kidnapping, threatened torture, soulmates.

Lastly, please note that I am **British** and this book is written in **British English**. There are variations in the language between the US and British English.

Happy Reading!

Selina x

PROLOGUE

THE MORRIGAN

*S*omewhere else...

Although we were cast out, not everything changed. A court of fae still surrounded me. Laughter continued, and my people still lived their lives. To them, it didn't matter that a barrier stood between us and the rest of the Thirteen Realms.

A barrier that took a lot of effort.

Centuries of work to find the right people, and for what? Three simpering gods to wedge a foot in the door and hog the energy. All while they trapped my warriors between the Veil.

Gods didn't need access to humanity to feed their powers. We simply required belief, and I had enough of that in my court. Yet some of my brethren weren't content with that. They wanted more, and I refused to give it to them.

But as much fun as I experienced toying with their efforts to bring down the barrier for good, I couldn't shake the need for... something.

My court happily danced and drank around me as though there wasn't a waste field beyond my walls. Two hundred years ago, I would have found pleasure in their joy.

Now, I couldn't stop my mind from wandering back to how horribly wrong my carefully laid plan went.

When the doors locked, with me on the wrong side, and the other gods discovered witches had trapped us, they turned to outright assaults on the barriers. I snorted, remembering the sight of it. No matter how despondent I became with waiting, their stupidity would never fail to amuse me. Gods wasting their reserves to attack an impenetrable barrier.

None of us possessed the power to sift through it. I'd made sure of that. Despite knowing that, they'd still tried.

When that failed, the infighting started.

And all the while, I watched, comfortable in my tower above it all, protected by my connection to the earth and my flock.

I could repair the damage, but the earth whispered to wait.

So I did.

For three hundred and fifty-five years, I have waited for my twelve warriors to escape their prison and finish the job. The gesture had grown fake and keeping my boredom secret had become difficult. Impatience passed centuries ago. Then came rage and now, I'd reached a level of apathy that concerned even me.

Everyone stopped as I rose. Every eye in the room burned against my skin. I smiled, because I always did. I left the ballroom and walked down the guarded corridors with well-practised purpose, determination in my stride even though I had no destination in mind. Beyond the swish of my gown and the clatter of my heels, silence reigned.

When I reached my chambers, my ravens waited, all three of them perched on their stands, eying me with quizzical tilts of their heads.

"Don't look at me like that," I said, my tone a little defensive. "I put in an appearance. They'll be fine without me."

It didn't appease them, but I ignored them, turning instead to the thing I now realised had been whispering to me for the last hour.

The mirror took up the entire back wall of my walk-in wardrobe — I might be trapped, but a woman needed her treasures. The frame glittered with a dirty gold that spoke of age and an ornate finish that showed ancient craftsmanship. But the glass was anything but old. It shimmered no matter the light. Power imbued it, and not mine.

The stranger thing? I couldn't remember acquiring the piece. It just turned up the day my men were captured and my plan stalled.

Ever since, it had shown me things.

Could it have news of my warriors?

The image cleared, and the moment of elation crashed.

Although it displayed men, the two before me bore no resemblance to the coven of twelve who served me. No, these two wore modern clothing, and though handsome, neither of them could compare to my men. They differed in both appearance and energy. One had an athletic build with sun-kissed blond hair and calm blue eyes. The other, with a shock of vibrant red hair and hazel eyes, seemed more awkward.

Stunning though they were, why had the mirror showed me them?

Then their conversation floated over me, as though carried on a breeze.

"Will you stop with the flicking?" The blond demanded, exasperation leaking from him. He lay on a sofa, sprawled out and uncaring of where his feet lay. "We've talked about this. There isn't a woman on the planet who would handle us, let alone him."

He hooked a finger to an armchair in the corner that contained a hulk of a man I had entirely missed in my first perusal. Shadows wrapped around him and something inside of me perked up.

"Okay, you've got me intrigued," I muttered to the mirror as I edged closer. "Tell me more."

An almost foreign feeling bubbled in my stomach. Giddiness. Excitement. Anticipation. Call it whatever the Annwn you wanted. I hadn't felt it in aeons.

As they continued bickering amongst themselves about their chances and the need for hope, I eyed the mirror critically.

It couldn't have responded to me.

The very idea of it was absurd.

And yet... every time the boredom grew unbearable, the mirror gifted me a distraction.

My eyes narrowed on the three men before me. *What distraction did they pose?*

I couldn't imagine any of them working for my brethren. The air of optimism would have dissolved from their auras within weeks of getting into bed with one of them.

"I refuse to believe the goddess would abandon us like that," the red-haired one said with a determined glint in his hazel eyes, "and I'm not going to stop swiping until we find her."

The other two groaned, but I leaned closer. *Goddess?*

"Which goddess would that be, child?" I murmured to myself.

All three were witches, that much I could ascertain. The flavour of their magic eluded me, no doubt thanks to the barrier.

Once upon a time, I had been *the* voice of all witches within the Thirteen Realms. They called to me with every ritual, fuelling me, feeding me as they called for my vengeance and directed my warpath.

Those calls had reduced to whispers over the years, voices so soft, I could believe them nothing more than the wind.

"The Morrigan wouldn't concern herself with the likes of me, Finlay," the raven-haired one encased in the shadows said. "Leave it be, for once."

The note of despondency in his voice quieted the

race of my thoughts. It triggered an answering pang of hopelessness in my chest. A pang I detested. It suggested me weak.

Witches invoking my name could not be blinded with anguish.

"This one doesn't have the first clue who I take an interest in," I growled, glaring at the raven-haired man now.

Tall, dark and stormy had always been my preference, but the darker the soul, the more violent their reactions. *And I just adore a bloody massacre.*

"I'll show them."

"Leave it be, Morri," Ciara, the head of my raven guard muttered behind me.

I glanced over my shoulder at her, still in raven form, those beady eyes seeing more than I liked.

"How can I ignore a cry for help?"

A chuff sounded from Ciara's neighbour. My eyes narrowed on Aisling, laughing at me.

"You're not a matchmaker," Mara said, utter boredom cloaking her words.

I bit my lip, an idea sparking with the idea of it. Turning back to the mirror, I barely saw it, too lost in the possibility of it. *Matchmaker. Me?*

"Maybe not." I hummed, testing the idea over and over.

But it had worked on Lucifer. And it would be a handy failsafe in future, and until then… well, it would be remiss of me not to practise before bestowing such a gift on my warriors.

"The witches don't beg for my marks for nothing."

"They've forgotten it ever existed." Aisling clucked at me, her alarm rising.

"All the better to sew a little chaos." I smirked, my gaze now fixed on my first unsuspecting victims — *I mean gift receivers*. "Now, if only I could add a Witches Council member or two to the mix..."

I settled back against my bed and shut my eyes. Blocking out the peanut gallery of dissenting ravens, I forced it all out. Every zing of feeling inside of me quieted and I focused on them, on the threads of their essence I could reach.

My magic gripped them, gathered them up and raced off into the night, searching, hunting for the perfect match.

I grinned when I found her. A spitfire of a witch, bristling at the constraints of her life. Even better? She would be my first cog of chaos in the Witches Council's.

They'd locked away my warriors and turned my plans against me. They would rue the day they pissed off the Goddess of War.

CHAPTER ONE

RHYDIAN

*E*dinburgh, Earth…

"I'm telling you, I have a good feeling about this one," Finlay said, barely contained excitement leaking from him.

He strode down Rose Street, a bounce in his step that I couldn't quite master. No, I trudged through the shadows, wary of being seen by the Friday night revellers spilling out of the pubs. I might have also been a little reluctant to watch my friend get his hopes up again.

"And I'm telling you to rein in the hope a little," Knox muttered next to him.

"Or you could be brave and face the woman." Finlay grinned, a knowing glint in his brown eyes.

Knox didn't bother to respond. He didn't need to — women fell over themselves for him. With his unscarred, pretty-boy face, short blond hair, and baby blue eyes, they couldn't help themselves.

No, it was after they met the rest of us that things usually went south.

Finlay's lankiness hardly registered next to Knox's swimmer's build. Even so, both were approachable, even charming in their own ways. But then there was me — a hulking mass of muscle and shadow, radiating danger from every pore.

Our lack of female company had nothing to do with Knox or Finlay. Alone, women approached them eagerly, starry-eyed. Even Finlay's awkward charm drew them in.

Add me to the mix, though, and they invariably begged off. I tried not to let it get to me. I had enough demons clamouring to consume me without adding a stranger's rejection to the mix.

But sometimes, watching Knox and Finlay's easy interactions only highlighted how much of an outsider I was — even among my own friends.

"It's not me I'm worried about." Knox smirked, a teasing note weaving through his Scottish brogue.

Finlay side-eyed him but kept moving, weaving through the crowd like a pro. A lifetime spent in Edinburgh could do that to anyone. Bloke pulls out a bagpipe on Princes Street, and no one bats an eye. One o'clock guns go off, and only the out-of-towners react.

"Do I ask you guys for anything?" Finlay asked with a tone that set me on edge.

It's a trap, an alarm blared in my head.

Knox groaned. "Here we go again."

I shook my head at the idiot. We'd dragged ourselves out every Friday night for the last year to meet Finlay's latest catch.

Finlay spun around, catching Knox's arm to stop him. He speared us both with a serious look. "I haven't asked you for anything but this."

I shifted uneasily beneath that stare. He rarely got that serious, only when it came to us and the bond we imagined between us. The first day we met at university, we each felt this uncanny certainty that we belonged together. We'd never been able to figure out why, but we'd stuck together for ten years.

"I don't know why you're lumping me in with the problem." Knox shot me a frustrated look. "Some of us actually try, you know."

I glared at him. Just because I agreed it felt right to stay together didn't mean I had to get behind inviting a stranger in. Knox bared his teeth at me in response, their tips morphed into the fangs of a wolf.

"Put those away." I clenched my fists, barely controlling the urge to pull him into the shadows with me.

He shut his mouth but didn't look cowed. No, the little shit arched a brow, determination blazing in his eyes.

Finlay shot me a hard look over his shoulder. "Drop the dark and brooding act, Rhydian."

"Fine," I ground out. "Can we get off the street now?"

Just because I agreed did not mean I'd invest any emotion into the encounter. We'd met hundreds of women at this point. It never ended well for us.

Finlay grinned before he spun around. He led the way, merging back into the crowd.

I returned my focus to our surroundings and the many hiding places for my enemies to ambush me. If they ever figured out who I was.

We hadn't taken more than ten steps before my attention snagged on a fiery-haired woman rushing towards us with her head down. A fitted black skirt hugged her hips and legs, while a deep navy blue — my favourite colour — blouse draped her, hiding what instinct screamed would be a delectable body.

She tried to slip between Finlay and Knox but must have misjudged the space. Their shoulders touched, forcing Knox and Finlay to turn. She glanced up sharply, her beautiful green eyes clashing with mine for the briefest of seconds. I knew her. Her lips parted in surprise as she took the guys in, something heated flashing across her pale freckled face and then vanished.

"I'm so sorry," she said, forcing a grin. She gestured at herself. "In my own world."

She waited for the guys to laugh, tension radiating through her. Neither of them could do more than blink at her.

When they didn't respond in any way, she backed away, a crease forming between her brows. "Well, sorry again," she muttered.

"Did any of you feel..." Knox glanced down, his lips flatlining. He rubbed his chest with a puzzled look.

"Like she was familiar?" Finlay finished for him. "Yes, but from where?" He glanced between us.

"I feel funny," Knox whispered, his expression pinched.

Finlay paled and rubbed his chest too. With his dark red hair, his appearance quickly turned sickly.

"If you're both done with the weird, shall we get off the street?" I eyed every corner and vantage point, my entire body on edge, searching for an unseen enemy.

It paid to be on guard at all times. Especially when my two idiot best friends were making a target of themselves in the middle of a busy narrow, cobblestoned street while the light faded and faux gas lamps flickered to life.

Knox and Finlay doubled over, clutching their hearts, hissing in pain as they crumbled to their knees. People dodged them, openly gawking but not helping.

"What's wrong with you two?" I asked, exasperated.

Pain flared in my chest, so intense it ripped me from the shadows. Startled gasps rose around me, people reacting to my sudden appearance no doubt. I couldn't focus on them. The burning on my chest took every ounce of attention I had.

It seared through me, making my eyes water worse than any gunshot or knife wound I'd experienced. It cut so deep I could imagine it touching my soul.

I tugged my t-shirt away from my chest and peered down the neck. A glowing purple mark had appeared like a tattoo. Curved tips intersecting a central circle.

Beyond the simple mark, something shifted inside of me. My shadows glamoured around my fingertips, desperate for something… someone. I frowned at the unbalancing ache in my chest.

As the pain lessened and the mark stopped burning, the glow settled into a black ink… or as ink-like as a supernatural mark could become.

"What the fuck is that?" Knox asked, his voice shaking.

He stared down his shirt too, a deep furrow between his brows. Both he and Finlay glanced up at me, their eyes wide, both of them unmistakably shaken. One look and I snapped out of the shock.

"We'll discuss it when we get home." I stood, straightening to my full six-foot-five height.

My gaze roamed the street, searching for signs of danger, a witch who might have cursed us.

No one appeared to pay us any mind. That did nothing to soothe my raging shadows.

"But what if—" Knox's mouth snapped shut at my sharp glare.

"Not until we get home," I bit out through a clenched jaw.

He started walking again, but Finlay continued to stare down the street with a familiar glint of fascination in his brown eyes.

"What is it, Fin?"

He pursed his lips and I could almost see the cogs turning in his mind. "I don't know… yet."

But he would.

Although soft in all the ways I couldn't be, Finlay could be just as dangerous. His abilities gave him just as much reach as my shadows, but his brain would always trump my strength. If anyone would figure out our sudden predicament, he would.

At least one good thing came of it. We didn't have to suffer through another rejection.

"Don't look so relieved, Rhydian." Finlay's eyes narrowed on me, almost like he'd heard me. "This only delays our date. It'll still happen."

Knox chortled at him while I settled for a silent glare. *We'll see about that.*

CHAPTER TWO

EDIN

*O*ne *week later*

"I'm so glad you called," I said, sliding onto the bar seat next to my best friend. Just the act of sitting down helped some of the tension drain from my shoulders.

That did not mean I started being careless. No, after the week of insanity I'd experienced, I'd never be careless again.

"I mean my reasons were entirely selfish, but you're welcome." Veronica grinned at me, a straw pressed to her lips and a devilish glint in her brown but blue-rimmed eyes.

To a non-witch, the sight would have been unnerving.

Only the most powerful among our kind displayed our power in the eyes. Veronica had graduated number one in her Vitakinesis class. She'd almost ranked on a par with her teachers for healing.

I should have expected her to see right through me the second I sat down.

"Why do you look like you've had a hellish week?"

A strained chuckle slipped from me. "Maybe because I have?"

I waved to the bartender while she continued to stare at me. Sparks flared on my fingertips. I clenched my fist, snuffing out the flames before the Witchkind in the room could notice. After a week of this nonsense, I'd about reached the end of my tether.

In the twelve years since my magic surfaced, I had never experienced such a loss in control. My flames had taken to me with a purr where others spent years fighting to control the inferno inside of them.

Until last Friday.

I snuck a glance at Veronica, stupidly hoping she hadn't noticed.

She stared at me. "Why did you do that?"

I leaned towards her, ducking my head, and hissed; "I didn't."

"What do you mean you didn't?" Her eyes widened and alarm flared in her tone.

"It's been like this for a week." I snuck a glance around the room, assessing if anyone in the busy bar could overhear us above the trickle of music and the clatter of drinks on the bar. "I don't know what's wrong," I whispered, momentarily distracted as my eyes clashed with a pair of dark green ones in the darkened corner of the room.

They almost glowed, shadows swirling through them. I could only make out the silhouette of their owner, his frame too cloaked in shadows. And those eyes… they were glued to me. *What the hell?*

I blinked, and they vanished.

Every inch of me tensed up and I straightened, frantically searching the bar for a hulking man making his retreat. No one moved.

The bartender cleared his throat, dragging my suspicious attention away from the corner. I ordered while Veronica bit her lip, concern for me clear in her gaze.

"Maybe it's just stress," she said when a drink sat on the bar top in front of me and the bartender had moved away to serve someone else.

Her manicured hand landed on my forearm, squeezing briefly before heat flooded me. The full body ache of too many sleepless nights faded. The pressure in my forehead cleared and the burn of my puffy eyes dissolved. For the first time in days, the ball of anxiety sitting on my chest eased and I could take a deep breath.

"That'll at least give you some breathing room," Veronica muttered. Her brow furrowed and her lips pursed. "But I can't help with the control issue. That's so weird."

My shoulders slumped. "I keep thinking I've been cursed."

"Maybe it's time to call your brother."

"Nope." I shook my head hard. "Nothing's serious enough for that."

"Edin, lovely, he's the best curse breaker in the country." Practised patience filled Veronica's voice. "If anyone can figure out what's wrong with you, it's him."

"I'm not that desperate." Yet.

I hadn't spoken to Hamish in four years. Not since I'd graduated from university and accepted a secretarial position with the Witches Council. When my conspiracy theory-obsessed brother found out, he blew up. We'd never fought before that, but the divide between us now would take more than a white flag phone call to fix.

"It's not an option." I forced a sunny smile to my lips, channelling the Edin of a week ago who liked her job and didn't fear leaving her flat. "Change the subject. How are you?"

For a second, Veronica's expression hardened, resisting the change. Then she shook it off, silently conceding defeat. For now. I knew her too well to think she wouldn't be calling me tomorrow morning to push a little more.

"Great. My new assistant is gorgeous, if a little green." The devilish sparkle returned. "You know, I think he's single, and he's totally your type. I could set you up?"

"I'm good."

Veronica chuckled. "Don't speak so fast. I haven't shown you a picture yet."

Sighing, I shifted in my seat. Eyeing the Moscow mule before me, I resisted the need to down the whole thing, too scared of what might happen if I touched it.

I loved spending time with Veronica, I really did. But when she got her teeth sunk into a juicy bone, the woman would not quit. *Maybe there's a touch of wolf in her ancestry.*

"Maybe this control issue is your power putting its foot down," she said, her tone a little too amused.

"Don't be ridiculous."

"I'm not. I think." She frowned for a second before her determination flooded right back. "There are stories of a time when the powers were more sentient, guiding their witches. Maybe it never went away."

"Please don't compare my problems to an old wives tale." I dragged a hand through my unruly auburn hair. For a couple of days, I'd been terrified to touch it, fearing my power would set *me* alight. "Anyway, we were meant to be changing the subject."

"Can I help it if your supernatural drama is more intriguing than my twelve hour shifts in A&E?" She smirked but failed to mask the concern in her eyes. "Between your love life and this power issue, it beats dealing with the usual parade of injuries and ailments. Besides, the last time I saw you, you were going on about a hollowness in your chest. Maybe it's all connected — and who knows, a little romance might just be the cure you need."

"And what do I say when I burn the hair from their bodies?" I snorted. "Sorry, I slipped?"

"It would bring a new meaning to fire play." Veronica chortled, her musical laugh floating over the bar and drawing the eye of every heterosexual man in the room.

Nearly all anyway.

Two of them resisted her. A blond with broad shoulders that stretched his burgundy shirt to its limits, and a thinner but equally gorgeous guy with hair a darker shade of red than mine.

In fact, their eyes seemed to be fixed on me.

Their attention burned against my bare skin, touching me deeper than the surface. Heat pooled inside of me, pulsing and needy. My gaze clashed with the blond's and he lifted his drink to me, a slick, flirty smile curling his lips.

A peculiar sensation washed over me. Something about them seemed... familiar. An inexplicable feeling of déjà vu tugged at the edges of my mind.

"Honestly, maybe it's just time for you to take a chance, put your heart out there again." Veronica's voice filtered through the fog of lust unfurling inside of me. "If it helps your control and fills that emptiness you're so concerned about, then isn't it worth at least trying?"

"I don't think it has anything to do with my love life." Or lack thereof.

Magic doesn't care how much sex we have or how fulfilled we are. It's about ancestry, energy and strength. I had all three... until now.

"Besides, where am I meant to meet a decent guy? As much as I enjoy my job, I wouldn't date any of the guys I work with."

Veronica glanced around us and then her attention returned to me with an arched brow. "There's like twenty hot, single guys in this bar right now." A wicked grin curled her lips. As if I would pick up some stranger in a bar.

"Yeah, yeah, I know." Her phone rang in her purse. As she fished it out, she continued, "I'm just saying that if it were me lighting things on fire unexpectedly, I'd want to try everything, no matter how out of the box."

She answered the call, leaving me to stew in her advice. I stared at my untouched drink, daring myself to be brave and touch it. A strong shot of alcohol would go a long way to clearing my worries…

My fingers didn't so much as twitch, fear holding me firmly in its grasp.

So maybe she had a point. I'd never let fear hold me back before. For my entire life, I'd charged into every situation with practised calm. I always had a plan and could shift directions with ease.

The hesitation I felt now fit wrong. It clung to me too tightly, suffocating all my trust in myself. My fire control had crashed out a week ago, but the hollowness Veronica obsessed over had haunted me for close to a year.

I'd tried to block it out, but the longer it lasted, the more unsettling it became.

Ignoring it hadn't gotten me anywhere. Maybe I should try some of Veronica's methods. If I could trust anyone to lead me right, it had to be my best friend, the doctor who could literally see inside my body with a touch.

"I'm so sorry, I have to go." Veronica downed her drink and shifted off her barstool. She gave me an apologetic smile. "An emergency's come up at the hospital and they need me to consult."

I eyed her empty cocktail glass. "Do they know you're out?"

"Yeah, but I'll force all that out of my system on the taxi ride over." She tugged me into a hug. "Raincheck, yeah?" At my nod, she relaxed a little and grabbed her purse. "Think about what I said. You've got nothing to lose by testing things."

With that she raced out the door, leaving me to fend for myself amongst the Friday night cocktail crowd. I eyed the drink again. *It would be silly to brave busy George Street only to not drink anything...*

I took a deep breath and reached for the small metal mug. Condensation had formed on the pitted material. My fingers wrapped around it, lifting it with care. Trepidation swept through me as I tried not to slosh it all over the bar. The liquid level had risen considerably with the melting ice.

So good so far.

I blew out a shaky breath and took a big gulp, relieved when the cup held its shape.

"Mind if I sit here?" A man asked beside me.

I nodded before fully turning to take him in. The blond slid onto Veronica's vacant stool. The redhead stood behind him, eying me with barely restrained interest.

No matter how safe I felt in Edinburgh, sometime during uni, I'd decided that frequenting bars alone would only lead to trouble. I didn't have premonitions the way some witches did, but when I got that hit years ago, I'd taken it to heart.

I waited for the pang of unease to hit me.

With the pair of them smiling at me, alarms should have blared in my head.

Nothing happened.

Well, that's a lie.

Liquid splattered to the bar as the metal of the mug crumpled and melted in my grip. I dropped it with a startled gasp.

It shouldn't have surprised me. The sting of sadness definitely shouldn't have dug its claws into me. I'd been expecting it. Yet I still felt bad about the destroyed cup, about my terrifying loss of control.

The guys swept in, grabbing napkins and dabbing up the mess. All the while I stared at it, dejected, lost… and shifting too close to the edge of reckless desperation.

"I'm Knox," the blond said, flashing me that heart-stopping smile again, revealing a small dimple in his left cheek. "This is Finlay, and…." He glanced over his shoulder, stalling at the crowd behind him. Shaking his head, he refocused on me. "What if I told you I could help you with that little problem?"

My brows furrowed as his gaze dropped to my clenched hands. He couldn't possibly know… then I spotted the ring of yellow around his blue irises.

What did yellow mean?

I'd known this once upon a time…

It doesn't matter.

I chose to play dumb. "What problem?"

Knox smirked and leaned forward. "Your uncontrollable need to burst into flames, of course." His voice dropped, his Scottish brogue brushing over nerves that perked right up and sent a shiver down my spine.

And then his words registered.

I stiffened. "I don't have a—"

"It's okay, Firefly. We can help you," the redhead, Finlay, whispered.

I studied them both, Veronica's words echoing in my ears. They weren't giving me creepy vibes. If anything, they felt strangely familiar.

Their proximity alone made my power settle down. It purred in my chest for the first time in months.

"How?" The word fell from my lips, almost lost in the noisy bar.

"A kiss," Knox said as if it were nothing at all.

Surely not.

"I promise it will help."

"I don't know you." My gaze roamed the pair of them, taking in the details I couldn't make out across the bar.

A playful glint danced in Knox's blue eyes, matching the confident quirk of his soft, kissable lips. It was at total odds with his friend's quiet energy. Finlay's freckles added a touch of boyish charm. He smiled but there was a tension running through him that made him seem uneasy, almost out of place in the bustling bar, as if he belonged in the quiet company of books.

Magic clung to them as it did all witches, only the flavours changed to match our powers, just as our eyes did — Knox's felt dynamic and shifting, while Finlay's had a steady, grounding quality.

But the most striking thing? I felt safe.

Both men exuded an oddly comforting energy, like a

warm blanket on a cold night. It was as if just their presence soothed the restless flames inside me.

"How do I know your promises mean anything?"

"You don't." Knox leaned against the bar, while his
soft gaze devoured me. "You just have to trust your gut,
Sparky."

Sparky. Firefly. No one had ever given me a nickname and two strangers felt they could? Even more
surprising, I didn't feel the need to bristle. The attention
washed over me, wrapping me up in a blanket of intimacy I should have wanted to reject. The half-hearted
words to do so froze on my tongue.

"Okay," I said, shocking myself.

It took a moment for my agreement to register with
Knox. Then he grinned and his icy blue eyes lit up with
self-assured confidence.

He leaned forward and reached behind me, applying
pressure to the nape of my neck. He tugged me forward,
slanting his mouth across mine. My breath got stuck in
my throat before he could steal it.

Our lips met, and everything inside of me stopped.
The quiver of volatile power shivered and froze, before
surging in a manner that would have terrified me
seconds ago.

Only it didn't feel dangerous.

Knox kissed me tentatively at first, almost like he
expected me to pull away. But then our powers began to
mingle. Mine seemed to roll over, purring beneath the
onslaught of his presence. Every ounce of caution
drained from me as I basked in the wonder.

He increased the pressure, devouring me with long, drugging kisses best saved for private spaces.

Even so, I couldn't make him stop. Wouldn't dream of it.

The spicy taste of an Old Fashioned invaded my mouth with his tongue, and I clutched his shirt, trying to drag him closer. Every fibre inside of me seemed to align, to shift and reform until all it wanted was more of the stranger.

Beyond that, I almost wept at the achingly sweet feeling of the hole inside of me shrinking. *What in the goddess is this?*

CHAPTER THREE

FINLAY

*M*y Firefly blinked at Knox, absolutely dazed. She touched her kiss-swollen lips, a look of absolute shock flitting across her face. Then her brows furrowed and everything inside of me stilled.

Did it work?

I'd spent four days digging through the university archives, hunting for a single whisper of our marks. All kinds of terrifying scenarios ran through my head until I unearthed a book most witches had forgotten existed. A book that probably should have been locked away in the Witches Council's vaults beneath the castle.

The mark on our chests turned out to be a *serch bythol*, a symbol of eternal love and connection that The Morrigan had once bestowed on her most loyal followers. It supposedly tied us to another: our soulbond.

We couldn't figure out how we'd ended up with it,

but given our shit luck at finding a partner to accept us all, I had no intention of questioning it.

If I focused hard enough, I could just make out the flicker of the thread connecting us. That tiny piece of power had already started to fill in the hollow hole in my chest. The feel of it, eating away at my hope, had started to drive me mad. It had become a constant buzzing at the back of my mind, the fear that something important had slipped through our fingers and now we would suffer the consequences.

"How did you do that?" she asked, awe filling her voice.

She stared at her fingers, her perfectly normal, non-fiery fingers. Granted, if the book was to be believed, we had inadvertently *caused* her power imbalance. I refused to let that detail snuff out the warmth spreading through me. Not when I could almost touch my dreams.

"Seeing as I've saved you from mass destruction, do I get to know your name?" Knox's brows rose, that flirty I-know-you-want-me smile curving his lips.

"Edin," she said after a brief hesitation.

Knox propped his chin on his hand, acting the total smitten fool. "Such a pretty name."

My power flared in my chest, delivering knowledge I hadn't known I'd need.

Fire. Place of Pleasure.

Beautiful and fitting.

"Now that we're properly introduced." Knox grinned as Edin's gaze dropped to his lips. "Come join us at our table and we'll tell you everything we can."

Edin chewed her lip, her gaze dancing between us.

"I just settled your power." Knox leaned forward, dropping his voice to a sultry whisper. "Would I do that if I meant you harm?"

Her focus wandered again before she flushed and righted herself.

"Sparky, you could toast me faster than I could change shape." He grinned. "Even with a little power imbalance."

Her eyes narrowed at that and her spine straightened. "Fine. One drink and then I'm gone."

I bit my cheek to stop my instinctual protest from slipping out. We just found her. I had no intention of letting her go so easily.

I hadn't been able to parse her name from any of the witch registries. Someone had made our witch practically untraceable, but we had an in. Nothing seemed to block the threads. Something I intended to thank the goddess for at every turn. We wouldn't have found her without it.

Edin slipped off her stool and followed us through the crowded bar to our still-empty table. She paused in front of it, confusion flashing through her expressive green eyes.

An empty table in the middle of a busy bar would look weird, since she couldn't see the giant of a man surveying the room.

I met Rhydian's watchful gaze with a silent demand. He sighed and let the shadows roll back. She gasped, finally seeing our fearless protector. *In his eyes, anyway.*

Every year, his paranoia only grew. With his shadowing capabilities and sheer size, it made sense that he slipped into the shadier side of the witch world.

That didn't mean his enemies knew who he was or would ever find us though.

That knowledge did nothing to assuage his paranoia.

"How did you do that?" she asked, her feet firmly planted.

Knox chuckled. "One thing at a time, Sparky." He gestured to the booth. "Why don't you sit down and we'll share it all?"

"I specialise in Osmosis," I said, keeping my tone light and friendly. No need for me to add to Knox and Rhydian's intensity. I slid into the booth, settling at Rhydian's side. "There's nothing I can't pull from a book."

Nothing I couldn't plant in someone else's mind either. But I kept that to myself. It made people uneasy.

"That's rare, isn't it?" Edin asked.

I restrained the need to puff out my chest like a preening fucking peacock. Instead, I nodded.

She stared at me for a moment, her indecision weakening.

I could just slip into her mind and share most of the facts with her, let her believe the truth, that she would always be safe with us.

Except I'd never forgive myself.

In the end, I didn't need to prod her. Determination hardened her expression and she slid in on the opposite side. She stopped with half a foot between her and Rhydian. Then Knox sat down next to her, blasting her careful distance to smithereens.

Edin glanced at him, brows rising at his brazenness. "You mentioned changing shape..." She tilted her head, considering him. He flashed her his favourite wolfy smile and she frowned. "Are you a wolf shifter?"

His teeth morphed back to normal, but his eyes sharpened, turning yellow, while the pupils elongated to that of a cat's. The demonstration only confused Edin further.

"I'm a witch shifter, gorgeous. There's no animal shape I can't assume." He leaned forward, a devious twinkle in his human eyes. "But if you've got a thing for wolves, I'll happily let you play with mine."

Rhydian rolled his eyes.

Edin snorted. The amused crease of her eyes relieved me no end.

"Down boy." She placed a hand on his chest, pushing him away.

Knox's stiffened, but not in affront. His head fell back in delight and I dug my nails into the leather of the booth, fighting to keep myself still. That tiny innocent touch did something to him and I desperately needed to know what.

Why can't I read people?

It seemed unfair that I could plant ideas but not read a person's mind.

Edin either didn't notice or she chose to ignore it. Her attention turned to Rhydian with a glimmer of curiosity.

"What about you?" she asked, her voice low, almost like she feared spooking him. Her gaze travelled over the darkness hovering behind him. "I've never seen someone step from the shadows like that before."

Rhydian's jaw shifted, but he didn't respond. The big oaf acted like he hadn't even heard her. *What the actual fuck!*

"Rhydian's a shadow master," I said, the words bursting from me a little harshly.

He scowled at me and Knox chuckled. I ignored them both, focusing only on Edin. Rhydian could shout at me later, but no way would I let him ruin this for us.

"He can control them, make more, cover himself and things, or,"—I pressed my elbows against the table as I leaned forward with a conspiratorial grin—"and this is my favourite part, he can travel through them."

Edin studied him, her gaze raking over his body and the space around him. "That's why I couldn't see you earlier," she muttered almost to herself.

"Yeah, he likes to hide away in the shadows."

Rhydian growled. I rolled my eyes but should probably have quit while I was ahead.

"Say it a little louder, Finlay," he ground out. "I'm not sure the assassin in the corner heard you."

We all glanced around the room. Unease spiked inside of me until I looked back at the smirking asshole.

"Real mature, Rhyd."

"So, what about you, Edin?" Knox asked, leaning in with interest. "What's your story?"

Edin smiled proudly. "I'm a secretary for the Witches Council."

The three of us exchanged a quick glance. How

ironic. She'd clearly drunk deeply from the Council's metaphorical Kool-Aid.

"That must be... interesting work." I forced a smile.

Edin nodded eagerly, oblivious to the tension that had settled over us. "Oh, it is! The Council does so much good for our community."

Another shared look passed between us, this one tinged with amusement at the situation's absurdity. Edin missed it entirely, too caught up in her enthusiasm for her employers.

Knox cleared his throat. "Enough about work." With a finger pressed to her chin, he turned Edin's attention back to him. "We have a proposition for you."

"What kind of proposition?" Her brow wrinkled, but the fascination in her eyes didn't dim.

"You saw what I could do with just a kiss." Knox bit his lip as his gaze dropped to her lips.

For a split second, Edin's blue eyes glazed over.

"Yes?" she whispered, her voice hoarse.

"Spend the weekend with us. Maybe we could cure you for good." He rushed through the words.

As confident as he had always been in his appeal, we weren't dealing with a normal, everyday situation. We didn't want to just pick her up. We wanted to keep her. And that would take finesse none of us was ready for.

"I don't know." Edin winced and then glanced around the table, her gaze sticking on Rhydian.

I bit my tongue against the need to berate him for jeopardising our chances. He couldn't have pretended to be sunny for an hour? Typical.

"You don't need to say anything right now," Knox

said, tone soft and coaxing. He placed his hand over hers on the table. Her attention fixed on the contact and she visibly swallowed. "Stay, have a drink with us, get to know us."

"Yeah. The night's young, Firefly." I smiled, willing her to see past the doubts and feel the air of belonging settling over us. I'd never felt so right in my life, not even when I met Rhydian and Knox.

Edin chewed her lip, weighing our offer. The suspense was excruciating — I felt like a man waiting for a jury to deliver its verdict.

CHAPTER FOUR

EDIN

*O*ne drink turned into two and then three. Time drifted away as I got lost in the three men surrounding me. Finlay and Knox kept me entertained, sharing their horrifying, yet funny, stories from their jobs at the Zoo and the University. I couldn't remember the last time I'd had so much fun.

The more time we spent together, the more natural it felt. Even Rhydian's silent brooding routine seemed to fit. I wouldn't have changed a thing.

You've got nothing to lose by testing things.

Veronica's words echoed inside my mind the entire time, daring me to be brave yet reckless.

But even as logic blared that going home with three strange men would be stupid, I couldn't deny Knox had calmed my power. I hadn't had a single splutter of explosive flames since. Their proximity alone seemed to help. My inner fire still burned bright, but it had almost curled up for a nap. A novel thing I'm not sure I'd ever experienced.

I also had this gut feeling that I could trust them.

Which in itself was absurd. I didn't do gut feelings.

Working for the Witches Council taught me to rely on facts and logic, even with magic. But sitting here, surrounded by these men and their attention, I found myself listening to my gut instincts instead. Something about them just felt right.

I trusted them and I liked them.

A weekend wrapped up in all of their attention sounded wonderful.

And it helped that I found all three of them attractive. I studied Rhydian. His massive frame and stoic expression screamed disinterest, but his emerald eyes told a different story. More than once, I'd caught him watching me, his gaze filled with an intensity that mirrored my own curiosity. Those stolen glances silenced the whispers of doubt in my mind.

Secure in their want for me, I let myself go and relaxed against Knox. Just enough to close the minuscule gap between us and soak in the press of firm muscle against my bare arm.

Silence roared around us as all three of the guys snapped their mouths shut. Finlay and Rhydian stared at the contact, flickers of envy in their eyes. Knox's gaze burned against the side of my face, but I steadfastly avoided looking at him.

Just because I'd found a grain of bravery to push us forward, that didn't mean I trusted myself not to flee.

I needed more time…

"How did you all meet?" I asked, desperate for a distraction to keep me from second-guessing myself.

I almost laughed as they shared warning glances.

"Was it bad?"

Knox chuckled. "If you count these two walking in on me…" He stopped, coughing awkwardly, and I gave into my curiosity.

I leaned away from him to take in his reddening expression while he glared at Finlay. Curiouser and curiouser.

"So it was bad?"

"Definitely. But it seems Knox has learned the meaning of appropriate." Finlay laughed, a delighted sound that made Knox tense. "We caught him in a compromising position on our first day in the dorms. We thought we were going to check out our shared living room…"

Rhydian pressed his twitching lips together, his dark and brooding mask cracking a little with the strain.

"I put a sock on the door," Knox grumbled. A sullen air settled over him and I couldn't help but smirk at the suave pretty boy.

"As if we knew what that meant." Finlay shook his head. "We were barely eighteen. Forgive me if we weren't as much of a player as you that early-on."

"But you were, eventually?" I asked, my eagerness plain to hear and see as I leaned forward, hanging on his every word.

Finlay pressed his lips together. "Let's just say

university was a time of… exploration, and leave it at that, shall we?"

I laughed. The idea of the scholarly Finlay indulging in the same wild antics as Knox tickled me. Rhydian remained stoic, but his eyes crinkled, betraying his amusement.

Knox laughed, bumping against me as he shook. "Careful, Fin, I'll happily spill *your* secrets tonight."

Finlay glared at Knox. "You were worse than me."

Worse how? I glanced between them, trying to figure secrets from their charged silence.

Knox's brows climbed. "Oh? Who set up our first foursome?" When Finlay only glanced at me, his lips clamped shut, Knox continued. "Not that I'm complaining, of course. That took balls for you back then."

He shifted, stretching his arm back and resting it on the seat behind me. He leaned in, his nose brushing my ear. That tiny touch sent shivers through me and made me ache with need.

"Finlay's powers come in very handy," Knox said, his voice low, making my nerves tingle. "You'd be surprised by the kinky shit he surprises us with."

"Knox!"

"What?" He leaned back far enough to meet Finlay's reproachful gaze.

Instead of his breath teasing me, his fingers moved in, toying with my hair, brushing lightly across my bare shoulder. I'd never been hyper aware of a man, but tonight that changed.

Finlay firmed his lips, glaring at Knox.

"Edin's not going to run away from your ideas, Fin."

Knox's fingers kneaded my shoulder, massaging the muscle and eliciting a moan.

My eyes fell shut on the bliss of it and my head lolled to the side, leaning into Knox's solid chest. I could get used to this. He rubbed his cheek against the top of my head, my hair tugging slightly as it caught in his stubble.

The more I touched him, the less empty I felt inside. Warmth filled me, making me want to curl up on the bench and take a much needed nap.

"Are you, Sparky?" he asked, his amusement melding with a barely contained groan.

Am I what?

I sat up, glancing around the table as if seeing their expressions would fill in the gaps.

Finlay stared at me, naked want flickering in his hazel eyes. Even Rhydian's indifferent mask had slipped, leaving me staring into his tense but heated expression. It made me want to crawl across the seat and straddle him, just to force him to give me more of a reaction.

I snuck a peek at Knox besides me. A smug smile curved his lips, but his blue eyes matched the tightness of his grip on my shoulder. Barely restrained desire clouded his expression.

"You'd like to experience the spicier side of Finlay's powers, wouldn't you?" he asked, his tone coaxing but rough.

"Yes," I whispered without thinking.

My gaze snapped to Knox, panic flaring inside of me. He grinned, but before any of them could respond, the bar menus on the table went up in flames. The guys reacted before my brain had fully grasped the sudden burn of heat. Shadows consumed the flames and, a second later, they sputtered out, leaving a charred mess.

I glanced at Rhydian, surprised. "You can steal the air from a space too?"

He stared at me, not blinking. His silence was all the confirmation I needed. Most witches had one speciality. To have two was virtually unheard of, and all the ones I knew of worked for the Witches Council.

"Clearly, my kiss at the bar wasn't enough," Knox muttered, drawing my attention back to him.

"What?"

My brain scrambled to catch up with the swift conversation change. What did kissing at the bar have to do with aerokinesis?

Then I noticed the flicker of light at the tips of my fingers.

"Shit." I squeezed my fist, snuffing out the flare.

Knox's frown cleared in the blink of an eye. He shrugged, his sexy smile falling back into place with ease. "I'll just have to try harder this time."

His grip shifted to the nape of my neck, tugging me harder against him.

Then he kissed me.

All of the breath left me at the first brush of his soft lips against mine. I tangled my fingers in his shirt, holding on for dear life as he devoured me for the second time tonight. I couldn't have stopped him even if I'd wanted to and, oh Goddess, how I didn't want to.

His fingers traced up my bare thigh. The teasing caress made me ache in all the best places.

I groaned at the cruelty of it, wishing I'd already said yes on their offer and we were somewhere else.

And then he reached the edge of my dress and kept going. His hand slid up the inside of my thigh while his lips and tongue reduced me to a needy mess, an expert at work. For seconds, I could only hold onto his shirt and let him sweep me away. When his fingers grazed my soaking underwear, I tensed, and reality crashed in.

I broke the kiss and tried to push him away. He leaned back, but held onto me.

"We can't," I gasped.

"Relax," Knox whispered in my ear. His hot breath caressed my cheek, triggering a shiver of excitement. "No one can see you."

I glanced around us. Silhouettes of people, but I couldn't make out any of their features.

"How?"

And more importantly, when? How long had we been shrouded by a wall of darkness?

"Rhydian doesn't like people seeing us," Finlay said, his tone both annoyed and grateful. "All they'll see is a dark corner."

While I processed that tidbit of information, Knox's fingers continued their teasing dance along the edges of my underwear. Was I really going to let Knox keep touching me? Was it really worth the risk of getting caught?

"Are you sure this will help with my magic?"

Knox's eyes locked with mine, gleaming with mischief. Rather than respond, he pressed his fingers against my clit through the soaking material, circling the bundle of nerves with a deft hand.

I groaned at not just the thrum of pleasure, but the way my magic purred in my chest. It made no sense. Witches couldn't affect each other's powers, not like this. Yet the heat at the tips of my fingers eased and the wild rush of power inside of me settled down even more than it had with our kiss.

His fingers slipped under my panties, stroking my pussy with just enough pressure that I couldn't help but moan out loud.

My head spun with pleasure and I prayed no one outside our booth could hear me as his fingers kept moving. Every touch sent sparks of pleasure shooting through me. All my worries faded away, and I sank into the moment, revelling in the sensation as Knox brought me closer and closer to the edge of sanity. The pleasure built with each stroke until I was clinging to him, begging for release.

My hips bucked against his hand without my permission, wanting more. Needing more. He smiled against my neck. His other hand held me tight against him. He kissed my neck and then his lips moved to my ear, grazing my earlobe with his sharp teeth.

This was too much, and yet not enough, all at once.

I panted, while his fingers never stopped their tantalising, relentless teasing. He knew exactly where and how to touch me until I was reduced to a quivering mess and then he'd slow down, dragging out my pleasure until I thought I'd go crazy from wanting more.

I groaned and the weight of eyes on me intensified,

drawing my head up. For a second, I thought I'd find the entire bar staring at me. No one's power was infallible. Instead, my gaze clashed with Rhydian and Finlay's heated gazes.

"Do you like being watched, Sparky?"

Knox's words sent a fresh wave of heat through me and my cheeks burned with embarrassment. It was wrong, so wrong, but god it felt good. He leaned forward until his lips were level with mine again. His mouth moved against mine as one hand roamed my body and the other remained firmly between my legs.

His thumb brushed my clit and I cried out as pleasure built inside of me. My eyes closed and my breathing hitched, all thoughts leaving my mind save for the man who was driving me wild with just his touch. Knox skillfully played me like an instrument, wringing out every drop of pleasure only to slow down just as I reached the pinnacle.

Fabric rustled, but I could barely think straight, let alone analyse the sound.

My eyes flew open at the press of a second pair of hands against my thighs. I glanced down, shocked to find Finlay kneeling beneath the table, smiling sheepishly up at me.

"You don't mind if Finlay has a taste do you?" Knox whispered against my ear before gripping my chin and turning my head towards him.

I swallowed hard and stared at him in disbelief. My heart raced as I slowly nodded yes. Knox's smile lit up his face.

"You won't regret that, baby."

His lips brushed against mine tenderly, and I relaxed into him. His fingers moved away from my opening, returning to rubbing teasing circles around my clit.

Finlay's hand slid up my thigh, pushing them wider to make space for his shoulders. A shiver of anticipation danced through me at the first puff of his breath against my slick pussy.

A gasp escaped me when Finlay touched me. His fingers explored me with a gentle curiosity that was altogether different from Knox's demanding touch. I jolted at the first caress of his tongue, almost jumping out of my skin. It was as though electricity passed through me from his tongue to the depths of my core. And then he began to lick, slow and deliberate at first, before picking up pace as I gasped and squirmed.

My hands found their way into his hair, clutching at the soft strands as his mouth moved over me. His fingers were there too, slipping inside me, moving expertly in time with his tongue. And all the while Knox kept teasing my clit, matching Finlay's pace in a rhythm that had me writhing beneath them both.

Their touch, the press of his tongue, the circling of Knox's fingers — it was all too much. But Goddess, did it feel incredible.

A moan tore from my throat, much louder than I intended. I could hear the hushed music and muffled laughter of people in the bar, but I was past worrying. I trusted Rhydian to keep us hidden and just felt.

The pressure built unbearably, my world narrowing down to the sensations created by Finlay's velvet tongue and Knox's insistent fingers.

Rhydian watched us, his eyes hooded with a look that was both protective and aroused.

"Edin," Knox whispered against my neck, "Come for us."

And I did.

My toes curled. I fell over the edge of ecstasy, my body shuddering against Knox. My nails dug into his thigh and Finlay's scalp, desperate for something to hold on to as I came apart.

You've got nothing to lose by testing things.

I bit my lip, studying the ceiling as I caught my breath and steadied my nerves. "About your proposition..." Three pairs of eyes snapped to me, the air growing thick with anticipation. I soldiered on. "One weekend. To see if you can help me regain control." I met each of their gazes. "I'm in."

CHAPTER FIVE

RHYDIAN

*L*etting a stranger into our space should have grated on me. I even braced myself to mask the discomfort of it. Instead, she slid into place among us as if she'd always belonged, a missing piece of a puzzle I hadn't known was unfinished.

While Finlay fetched drinks, Knox tried to ease the tension with his usual charm. Edin's laughter rang out, husky and warm, wrapping around my senses. The sound slid down my spine to pool low in my gut, making me yearn for something I could never have.

I glanced towards them and found her watching me through a fall of auburn hair, green eyes gleaming despite her obvious nerves. An open flame daring me closer even as it promised to scorch the flesh from my bones.

Damn my idiot friends for being right, and damn
The Morrigan for saddling us with this 'gift.'

None of my enemies had learned of Knox and
Finlay, and I worked damn hard to make sure it stayed
that way. But adding a fourth to the mix? And someone
bonded to us on a soul level, whose powers were
volatile? That would be a push too far.

I had no interest in tempting fate.

Unfortunately, neither Knox or Finlay shared my
concerns.

Knox hauled Edin onto his lap like he had every
right. She went easy, a soft noise slipping out as their
mouths crashed together, a clash of lips and tongues and
teeth that sent heat flooding through my veins. Something bitter and acrid coated my tongue — the taste of
jealousy, toxic and undeniable.

I tensed, slipping deeper into the dark corner of the
room. Shadows licked at my skin, ready to strike or
shield. To spirit me away from the gutting sight of Edin
tangled up in my best friends' arms.

Fingers sank into her hair. A hand cupped her ass,
kneading. Edin rolled her hips down and Knox groaned
into her mouth. The sound scraped along my nerves,
lighting them up until my teeth ached from clenching.

Finlay returned and placed the drinks on the coffee
table to be forgotten, his eager gaze fixed on them. He
settled beside Edin, close enough their thighs brushed.
He hesitated only a moment before leaning in to press a
soft kiss to her lips. Edin blinked in surprise, then smiled
against his mouth and kissed him back.

A jolt of something hot and unpleasant shot through

me at the sight. I shoved it down ruthlessly, ignoring the way my hands clenched into fists. They were free to do as they liked. I wanted no part of it.

Except I couldn't look away.

I shifted, uncomfortable with the sudden intimacy. It felt like an intrusion on something private — something I had no right to witness.

You're bound to her too, remember?

I wished I could forget. Maybe then the temptation would fade, and I'd be able to think straight.

Knox grinned, apparently unconcerned by the display of affection as he watched them with a heated glint in his eyes and a wry smile.

When they finally broke apart, Finlay rested his forehead against hers, both of them smiling with an ease that made my chest ache. Edin touched his face gently, her fingers lingering on his jawline before slipping away.

She drew back first, eyes gleaming. He watched her uncertainly, as if waiting for rebuke, but her smile only brightened. Reassurance without words that this — they — were alright.

"Sorry," Finlay mumbled. "I just… wanted to do that the moment I saw you."

"No need to apologise." Edin's gaze slid to Knox, a question in her eyes. His grin returned at full wattage as if in answer.

"Our Fin doesn't usually move so fast. You must have made an impression."

A faint blush stained Edin's cheeks at the praise, probably remembering how Finlay had already tasted her at the bar. "The feeling's mutual."

Knox laughed. "Good to know we're all on the same page then." His arm tightened around her, hand coming to rest on Finlay's shoulder, binding them all together.

A unit. As we were meant to be.

I leaned back against the wall, pulse pounding in my ears. This was madness. Inviting a stranger in, giving her power over us, when any one of my enemies would kill to exploit such weakness.

And yet.

The thought of turning her away left me cold. They needed her. Needed her laughter and the light she brought to chase back the shadows. And she needed them, though she likely hadn't realised how much. Not yet.

I scrubbed a hand over my face, torn between frustration and resignation. We were damned, the three of us, from the start. Finlay's research said there was no escape. Once chosen by The Morrigan, it was a rejection we'd never shake off or the soulbond.

If this was meant to be a gift, it might be the cruellest yet. The future stretched before us, filled with promise and peril in equal measure, with this woman at its heart.

I almost snorted at the ridiculousness of it all. Finlay had been desperate to find our centre, and now that we had, the thought of getting too close filled me with dread.

I couldn't miss the way they clamoured to be near her. Knox's spacial awareness had totally evaporated at the bar. Had I not been my typical paranoid self, he would have driven Edin to orgasm with an audience and regretted it when it backfired on him.

If I lost control like that, it would get me and them killed.

Maybe if I maintained my distance, I wouldn't get lost in the desperate need to touch her.

Finlay slid a palm beneath her shirt, making her shiver and her head loll back to bare the delicate line of her throat.

Ripe for the biting. Marking. *Claiming.*

I jerked my gaze away, stomach twisting. Fucking stupid, to let it get to me. I'd seen them with plenty of women over the years. This shouldn't have been any different.

But watching them touch Edin, tasting her gasps and swallowing her sighs... it gutted me in ways I couldn't explain. Couldn't *reason.*

"Rhydian..." A husky rasp, full of too much sin for my blackened soul to hear.

My head snapped up. Edin watched me from beneath lowered lashes, amber eyes glowing in the dim light. Seeing right through me, down to the howling beast rattling its cage.

Knox lifted his head from her neck, teeth flashing white against kiss-swollen lips. "What's wrong, Rhyd? Too scared for a taste?"

I should walk away. Retreat to the chilly isolation that kept me sharp. Focused. *Sane.*

But my feet might as well have been welded to the floor. Trapped by the heated promise in Edin's eyes, the sway of her body as Finlay thumbed circles into the skin above her hip.

Knox smirked, his gaze flitting between me and Edin. "Fair warning," he stage-whispered to her, "he's the grumpy one." He jerked his chin toward me.

She glanced my way, eyes dancing with mirth, but also concern. "I'm sure I can win him over."

"You might be waiting a while. He rarely cracks a smile." Knox heaved a dramatic sigh. "Alas, we bear the burden bravely."

"Left to your own devices, you'd have burned down the city or started a war by now." The words slipped out before I could catch them.

Edin laughed again, the sound sliding under my skin as she cocked her head, studying me. I felt pinned in place by her gaze, netted by invisible strings.

Knox blinked in surprise, glancing between us before his grin turned sharper. Plotting, no doubt. I shouldn't have encouraged him.

"Hidden depths." Edin's smile eased the tense lines around her mouth, travelling all the way to her eyes. No longer braced for attack but leaning into Knox's side, at home in a way I hadn't expected. "A grumpy exterior masking a secret softie."

"Soft is one thing he's not." Knox slid a sly glance my way. "Isn't that right, Rhyd?"

I chose not to dignify that with a response. Let Knox play his games; I was only here to keep them safe. Or so I told myself.

Knox shifted his hips and she drew in a shuddery

breath, her spine arching. The unmistakable scent of arousal thickened the air, choking me with its potency.

Leave now. Before you fuck this up beyond repair.

My fingers clenched, unclenched. Shadows writhed around me, agitated by the pulse pounding in my skull.

"Don't," I said, voice like gravel. "Don't tempt me."

It's not safe, I didn't say. *I'm not safe.* The words stuck behind my teeth, lodged in my throat like a blade.

"Why?" Pretty lips formed the question, soft and pleading. "Why pull away when I can feel this... this *thing* between us?"

A flinch rippled through me before I could stop it. She didn't understand. Couldn't know the violent urges riding me, the red forever staining my hands.

I swallowed hard. "It's not a good idea. Trust me."

The wrong thing to say. Hurt flickered across Edin's face, there and gone. Before I could blink, she slid off Knox's lap. Took a trembling step toward me, heedless of the danger.

Alarm spiked, cold and vicious. I threw up a hand, voice cracking out like a whip.

"Don't. It isn't safe."

Edin froze mid-step. Behind her, Finlay and Knox wore matching frowns. A charged look passed between them, some silent conversation I couldn't follow.

"Of course it's safe," Finlay said, exasperated.

"Right. Go on." Knox gestured between me and Edin with a wicked smirk. "It's your turn. A harmless little kiss won't hurt anyone."

I glared at him but the glint in his eye dared me to take

up the challenge — to do what I had been wanting since the moment we met. To taste her lips and perhaps get lost in the sweet temptation of her embrace. But I knew if I gave in, there would be no going back; I wouldn't just be crossing boundaries, but jumping off cliffs into uncharted waters. Dangerous waters that could swallow me whole if I let it…

I wanted her with a fierceness that shook me to the core and left me dizzy. But I couldn't give in to it.

So instead I stepped back, shaking my head. "No." My voice was hoarse, barely recognisable even to me.

Time seemed to hold its breath as Edin studied me, eyes wide and searching. I could feel her confusion as if it were a living thing between us, and for a moment I faltered under the weight of it.

But then Knox chuckled, and the spell broke. He winked at me knowingly before turning back to Edin with a lopsided grin that softened the disappointment in her eyes.

Darkness billowed out from me in jagged waves. The temperature plummeted, my shadows agitated beyond control. Edin shivered but held her ground, stubbornness etched into every line of her body.

I turned away, grateful for the darkness of the shadows that swallowed me up as I made my escape. But even then I could feel Edin's gaze lingering on me as if she could see straight through my facade and into my soul.

I gritted my teeth until my jaw ached. The cold embrace of my abilities beckoned, crooning sweet oblivion. Promising freedom from the want clawing beneath my skin.

Not her. Never her.

I wrenched away, a harsh sound punching from my lungs. Let the shadows sweep me up and away, scattering thought and form until only darkness remained.

And then solidity. My room, dark and musty. I sagged against the door, head thunking back against the scarred wood.

Fucking fool. Reckless *idiot.*

CHAPTER SIX

KNOX

*S*hadows swallowed Rhydian, leaving only a chill in the air and confusion on Edin's face. She stared at the spot where he'd vanished, hurt and rejection flickering in her amber eyes.

We should have known better than to expect a leopard to change its spots in a week.

I slid off the sofa and pulled her flush against me. She melted into my embrace with a sigh. I almost sighed myself. I would never get tired of that glowing warmth in my chest from just her touch. Finlay had moaned for years about the aching hollowness growing inside of him and to an extent, I'd understood, had felt it too. But I couldn't fathom what it would feel like to be whole.

I'd been fine as I was. Hadn't I?

With her pressed to me, I could admit the truth. I'd been a cocky fucking idiot.

I tipped her chin up, meeting her gaze. "Don't worry about him. He'll come around."

Edin bit her lip, uncertainty etched into the furrow between her brows. "Did I do something wrong?"

"No, no. Absolutely not." I smoothed my thumb over her cheek. "Rhydian's just a bit gun-shy, is all. Too used to staying hidden and watching our backs."

"He just needs a little adjustment time." Finlay joined us, his hand coming to rest at the small of Edin's back. A soothing touch, grounding her.

A weak laugh gusted from her, some of the tension easing from her frame. "Well hopefully he adjusts fast. The weekend will fly by."

I exchanged a loaded glance with Finlay over her head. Neither of us corrected her assumption that this would end after the weekend. For the next forty-eight hours, nothing else mattered but convincing her that there was something more than lust between us.

But later, when we'd exhausted her, Rhydian and I would be having words. I understood his reservations, truly. But nothing, *nothing* justified putting that look on our witch's face.

"How about we focus on something a bit more... pleasurable, hmm?" I slid my hand down to cup her ass, giving a suggestive squeeze. Edin gasped, her eyes darkening with rekindled hunger.

"I like the sound of that."

Finlay hesitated, his expression torn. "Why don't you go ahead and get started? I'm going to check on Rhydian, then I'll join you both."

I rolled my eyes, unable to hide my exasperation.

"You're wasting your breath. He'll come around when he's ready. No point in pushing him."

"I know, but—"

"Look," I cut him off, "if you want to waste your time, be my guest. But I've got much more interesting things to focus on." I smiled at Edin, threading my hands into her hair. The silky strands slipped through my fingers as I gently massaged her scalp. "Isn't that right, Sparky?"

Edin's eyes fluttered closed for a moment, a soft sigh escaping her lips. When she opened them again, her gaze was heavy-lidded and filled with desire. She leaned into my touch, a small smile playing on her lips. "Definitely more interesting," she murmured, her voice husky with want.

Finlay sighed but nodded, his gaze lingering on Edin before he turned away. "I won't be long," he promised, then disappeared down the hallway.

I turned my full attention back to Edin, my hands skimming her sides. "Now, where were we?"

Rhydian might be content to deny this — deny *her* — but I'd had my fill of noble idiocy.

Edin was *ours*, and it was time we showed her exactly what that meant.

I claimed her mouth in a searing kiss, licking past the seam of her lips to taste her moan. She opened beautifully, inviting me deeper as my hands skimmed her sides, dragging her shirt up, inch by torturous inch.

We worked in tandem, stripping each other bare between fevered kisses and worshipful caresses. My mouth mapped a path down the elegant column of her throat, teeth scraping gently. Marking her. A primal part of me growled in satisfaction at the blooming colour.

By the time we stumbled into my bedroom, clothes littered the floor behind us like breadcrumbs.

Edin crawled into the bed and lay down, her gaze roaming over my naked bodies with a flirty curve of her lips. I happily drank in the sight of her, sprawled across my sheets, acres of creamy skin flushed with want. My cock throbbed and impatience burned through me.

Goddess, I need her.

I climbed onto the bed, savouring the hitch in her breathing at the first brush of my skin against hers.

"Look at you." I traced the lush curve of her breast. "Laid out like an offering to the Goddess."

She shivered, back arching to seek more of my touch. "Touch me," she breathed, a plea and a demand. "I need—"

"Shh, I know." I soothed her with a kiss, a gentle counterpoint to the fire raging in my blood and the power unravelling in her chest. She was close to setting the room on fire.

Call me a sadist, but the image of us fucking while my bedroom burned around us did something for me.

"Let me worship you."

A soft moan lodged in her throat and she nodded. As if there had ever been any doubt that she wanted me.

"How do you want me the first time, Sparky?" I asked. My fingers grazed her hips and she jolted. "Shall I stretch your ass with a tentacle, get you ready to take two of us while I fuck you fast and hard?" My voice dropped as her eyes darkened at the thought.

A tentacle flared from my side, unravelling as I willed it into existence. The limb brushed against her, drawing a delighted gasp. It caressed her, tracing a line between her breasts, then circling a sensitive nipple.

She moaned at the sensation. Then a sucker latched on and her head fell back on a cry. Her hips shifted and the evidence of her arousal scented the air, teasing me.

I'd always loved my power, but if the Goddess were to appear before me right now, I would get on my knees and thank her for my animal affinities.

"Or," I made the tentacle vanish and she whimpered, her attention snapping back to me, "I could grow a knot and stretch you in a different way."

She swallowed hard, but the interest in her amber gaze only deepened.

"Tell me what you want, Edin."

"The first," she whispered, her voice hoarse. Her cheeks reddened, highlighting the smattering of freckles there. She met my gaze, shyness mingling with fascination. "Fuck me with your tentacles."

I grinned, letting a hint of fang peek through. My little adrenaline junkie. "As my lady commands."

Magic rippled over my skin. Shifting, changing, *becoming*. More tendrils unfurled from my sides, long and sinuous and glistening in the muted streetlights filtering into my bedroom.

Edin gasped, transfixed. Her gaze followed their undulating path as they crept up her calves, tickling the sensitive backs of her knees. "Oh, fuck."

"So responsive," I purred, fingers circling her nipple

into a straining peak. "You have no idea how perfect you are for us."

I directed a tentacle to slip between her thighs. It found molten heat, gliding through her slickness with obscene ease. Edin's head thrashed on the pillow, a choked moan pouring from her lips.

"That's it, love," I crooned, a second limb joining the first to circle her clit. Her hips bucked, chasing the pressure. "Let me make you feel good."

I feasted on her cries as my tentacles worked her mercilessly, twining and stroking and flicking, delving into her dripping pussy only to retreat and tease her slit, a maddening dance.

My head swam with her arousal, drunk on the slick slide of her flesh against my magicked own. Every shift and shudder telegraphed through the bond, an endless loop of sensation multiplied tenfold.

I lost myself to instinct, to the driving need to bring her higher. Harder. *More.*

A third tentacle slithered up the bed to brush her lips, tracing their lush shape before pressing past and into the wet silk of her mouth. Edin suckled instinctively, drawing a guttural curse from me as my hips rutted against the mattress.

I could feel the kitten lick of her tongue, hot and velveteen. The eager hollowing of her cheeks as she drew me deeper still.

It was rare that I got to stretch my powers like this. Most witches would run screaming if I so much as grazed them with a tentacle.

Not my pretty, perfect Edin though.

She stared back at me with pleasure glazed eyes and a burning need for more.

A growl tore from my throat, patience fraying. My tentacles pulsed, growing thicker. Longer. Stretching her *just* to the edge of discomfort.

Edin whimpered around her mouthful, lashes fluttering. Hips shifting helplessly as the tentacles plundered her, gliding and curling against fluttering inner muscles. Finding that spot that made her moan, high and needy.

"You want more of me, love?" I panted, grinding into the bed. The friction eased the ache in my cock, but only just. "Want me deeper?"

Desperate pleading, muffled but clear. I cursed again, eyes rolling back as a fourth limb snaked between her ass cheeks. Circling, teasing, drenching itself in the honey dripping from her pussy.

"Gonna fill this sweet hole too," I promised darkly, a vow and a threat. "Stretch this tight little rim until you're *sobbing* for it."

The tentacle breached her, pushing inexorably past the reflexive clench of muscle. Sinking into clinging heat, velvet-soft and searingly tight.

Edin gasped around the tendril in her mouth, a broken, almost pained sound that shot straight to my cock. I pushed deeper, slow and relentless, letting her feel every rippling inch. Savouring the flutter and squeeze of her body, welcoming me home.

"That's it," I rasped, blood roaring in my ears. Hips rocking in shallow, maddening thrusts as I fucked my own fist.

I lost myself to sensation then, to the slick slide and

filthy sounds of flesh on flesh. Tentacles pumping in synchronicity as they pistoned into her, wringing cry after broken cry from kiss-swollen lips. I set a brutal pace, every muscle in my body drawn taut and trembling with the need for *more*, to hear her shatter...

It crashed over her like a wave, sudden and inexorable. Her spine bowed, head thrashing as a choked scream tore from her throat. The sight seared itself into my brain, branding me to the bone.

Sensation ricocheted down the bond, a lightning strike that lit me up from the inside out. My curse mingled with her cry, half pain and half prayer.

*E*din merely hummed, a blissed-out little sound. Her eyes fluttered open, meeting mine with a lazy, satisfied smile that made my heart trip over itself.

I swallowed hard, my throat suddenly thick. Yeah, definitely in over my head with this one. I hadn't even gotten my dick wet yet and I already knew I'd never have my fill, not if I lived a thousand years.

Terrifying, that certainty.

The bedroom door creaked open, and Finlay slipped inside. His eyes widened slightly at the scene before him, a mixture of disappointment and arousal crossing his features.

"Rhydian's still refusing to join us," he said, his voice tinged with frustration.

I snorted, not surprised in the least. "Told you it was a waste of time."

He'd come around. He just needed space to adapt

and turn the scenario over a million times in his mind. Once he'd finished searching for all of the flaws and weaknesses and found defences for each one, he'd be on his knees begging her for a chance. I'd make sure of it.

Turning my attention back to Edin, I traced a finger along her flushed cheek. "What do you say, Sparky? Ready for round two?" I grinned, letting my gaze flick meaningfully to Finlay. "I'm sure we could convince Fin here to lend a hand... or more."

CHAPTER SEVEN

EDIN

"*G*oddess, how can you do... that... to me and still look so rational?" I asked, my voice embarrassingly breathy.

I stared up at Knox through half-lidded eyes. I struggled to string thoughts together, my mind still clouded with the afterglow of the most intense orgasm of my life.

Knox chuckled and smirked down at me. "Easy. You make me ravenous."

I sighed contentedly, my body still convulsing gently from the aftershocks of my previous orgasm. Ravenous was the perfect word to describe how much I wanted them. It was illogical, but I couldn't seem to care.

I craved so much more — more of their touch, more of their passion, more of the connection I felt with them. But even as I revelled in the afterglow, I couldn't shake the feeling that something was missing. Or rather, someone. Rhydian's brooding face flashed in my mind, and I felt an inexplicable pull towards him too. It was madness to want all three of them, wasn't it? And yet, the thought of being with just two felt somehow incomplete.

I pushed the confusing thoughts aside, focusing instead on the two gorgeous men before me. "Well," I said, a flirty smile playing on my lips, "if you're still hungry, I suppose I could offer myself up as the main course."

Finlay knelt between my thighs, his gaze fused to mine. A shy smile played on his lips, but there was an unmistakable glint in his eyes. "You know," he said softly, pushing his glasses up his nose, "there's a theory that pleasure is exponentially increased with multiple partners." His cheeks flushed slightly, but his voice grew bolder. "Perhaps we should test that hypothesis... thoroughly."

My jaw dropped, and a fresh wave of heat flooded through me. Was this the same shy, bookish man I'd met at the bar? Finlay's words, delivered with that perfect mix of academic interest and raw desire, short-circuited my brain. I couldn't find the words to respond, caught between shock at his boldness and a surge of excitement at this glimpse of his hidden depths.

My body, however, had no such hesitation. I nodded eagerly, a shiver of anticipation running down my spine at the thought of what was to come. His unexpected boldness sent a thrill through me. This man had depths I was eager to explore.

He lifted my hips and positioned himself at my

entrance, the head of his cock nudging me. As Finlay filled me, I couldn't help but wonder how it would feel with Rhydian here too. The thought should have exhausted me, but instead, it only fueled my desire.

Knox's tentacles tucked under me, lifting me completely off the bed. I gasped, my senses overloaded as Finlay continued to move deeper into me, his slow thrusts setting a decadent pace.

Suspended in the air by Knox's tentacles, I felt weightless, completely at their mercy. The sensation was both exhilarating and erotic, making me more sensitive, more aware of every touch, every caress.

Knox kissed me, his tongue delving into my mouth in a passionate dance that echoed the physical connection we shared. His tentacles breached my ass again, filling me in a way that bordered on the obscene, yet felt exquisite.

I whimpered into Knox's mouth, my body stretched taut between the two of them.

For a moment, I thought I saw a pair of intense green eyes watching from the shadows. My heart leapt, but when I looked again, there was nothing. Was Rhydian here, silently observing? The idea shouldn't have excited me as much as it did.

Their rhythm was perfect, each movement in sync, pushing me higher and higher. Knox's tentacles wrapped around me, caressing me, the suckers tugging at my sensitive skin and nipples. Finlay's cock filled me completely, his thrusts deep and slow, making me crave more.

Knox broke the kiss, his breath hot on my neck. "You like that, little witch? Being filled like this?"

I moaned, unable to form a coherent response. The sensations were too intense. My core tightened, another orgasm building.

Finlay stared into my eyes, his filled with determination and lust. "You're so beautiful, Firefly. I need to taste you," he said, his voice low and husky.

His cock slipped out of me, and a desperate denial fell from my lips before he lifted me higher, taking advantage of the tentacles holding me weightless. The protest died on my lips at the first flick of his tongue against my clit.

It sent shockwaves of pleasure through me.

"Finlay... oh my goddess," I moaned, my body responding to his tender touch.

His tongue swirled around my clit, flicking and sucking. I threaded my fingers through his hair, holding him to me as I revelled in the sensations.

Finlay's clever tongue drove me wild. Who would have thought this quiet librarian could reduce me to a quivering mess? Yet even as I revelled in his touch, a small part of me couldn't help but wonder how Rhydian's shadows would feel against my skin.

Knox's tentacles continued to work their magic on my ass and nipples, heightening my pleasure. His hand snaked up, fingers toying with my hair. He tugged gently, forcing my head back and exposing my neck. "You taste so sweet, little witch," he whispered in my ear, his breath hot against my skin.

Finlay's lips were still working their magic on my clit,

his tongue flicking and sucking in a rhythm that mirrored the throbbing of my heart. My body writhed against the tentacles, my hips bucking involuntarily as the intense pleasure washed over me in waves.

Knox's fingers traced the curve of my neck before he gently bit down. It was a possessive move, one that sent a shiver down my spine.

"Knox…" I moaned, my voice barely audible as Finlay continued to pleasure me.

"That's it, baby," Finlay murmured, his mouth never leaving my sensitive flesh. "Just let go."

Another orgasm crashed over me, a tidal wave of pleasure that left me trembling and gasping for air. I'd never been one for multiple orgasms but with these two, my body didn't want to stop.

If only Rhydian were here to share the moment.

Even in the heights of ecstasy, his absence was a bittersweet ache.

"You're so fucking beautiful like this." Knox whispered in my ear, his voice low and husky. "Your body responds to us so perfectly."

Finlay filled me again with one swift move. I moaned as he started to thrust, his pace relentless and deep as he chased his own release. Knox's tentacles continued their teasing of my nipples and ass.

"You're a fucking goddess, Edin," Knox said, his breath hot against my neck. "Look at you, suspended in mid-air, taking everything we give you."

My body writhed against the onslaught of pleasure, my hips bucking helplessly against the tentacles as Finlay neared his peak. His moans grew louder, more desperate, and I knew he was close. The thought of him coming inside me made my core clench. Thankfully, my pregnancy prevention spells were up to date.

"You're gonna make me come, Firefly," Finlay groaned, his cock swelling inside me. "You're so fucking perfect for us."

"Yes, Finlay... come for me," I whispered, my breaths ragged and uneven. The sensation of him filling me completely, the intensity of the entire experience, was almost too much to bear.

With a final, desperate moan, Finlay reached his peak. His cock pulsed inside me, releasing spurt after spurt of hot seed.

He pulled out of me and Knox took his place, uncaring that I was a mess of sweat and desire, panting and trembling.

Knox finally filled me with his thick, hard cock and I gasped, my body stretched to its limits. He began to thrust, his movements frantic but rhythmic, each stroke sending waves of pleasure coursing through my body.

"You feel so good, Edin," he moaned, his voice low and husky. "So fucking perfect."

I got lost in the whirlwind of pleasure, the coil tightening inside of me while he drove me mindless with need. His tentacles continued to torment my nipples and ass, heightening the intensity of each stroke as he claimed me.

"Knox... oh, Knox..." I moaned, almost screamed.

His hands gripped my hips, pulling me closer as his thrusts grew more intense, more frantic.

My muscles clenched around his cock, my body

convulsing in pleasure. I cried out, screams echoing around the room.

"Knox... I'm gonna... I'm gonna come."

"Come for me, Sparky," Knox growled, his thrusts becoming even more forceful. "I want to feel you milk me."

My orgasm hit, waves of pleasure crashing over me as I screamed out my release. Knox continued to thrust, his cock driving deep inside me as my body convulsed.

He let out a guttural groan as his own orgasm crashed into him, his body tensing as he released himself inside me. A wave of heat spread through me, mingling with the pleasure still coursing through my veins from my own climax.

As Knox's thrusts slowed, he lowered me to the bed, his tentacles stroking me one last time before fading away. He leaned over me, resting his forehead against mine, our breaths mingling raggedly.

"Holy fuck, Edin," he whispered, a hint of awe in his voice. "That was... beyond words."

I nodded weakly. Our bodies still trembled, the after-shocks of our shared orgasm lingering.

Finlay shuffled over, curling into my side. "Fuck, man," he said, his voice filled with satisfaction. "We just defied the laws of physics and made love to an extraordinary woman."

I couldn't do anything but laugh. As we lay there, catching our breaths, a sense of calm washed over me, wrapped in the arms of these two amazing men. The intensity of our session had left me feeling alive. We were tangled in a mess of limbs, drenched in sweat and satisfaction, but it was a beautiful sight.

They'd worked so well together. Their movements were almost choreographed.

But a tiny voice in the back of my mind whispered that if Rhydian were to step out of the shadows right now, I'd welcome him with open arms, exhaustion be damned.

"Can I ask you guys something?" I asked, my voice hesitant.

"Anything, Sparky." Knox rolled over, grinning at me. "We're an open book."

I took a deep breath. "What's the deal with... you three? I mean, this isn't the first time you've shared a woman."

Finlay blushed, but Knox just chuckled.

"But you're not... together?"

"Not romantically, no." Finlay shook his head. "It's more... complicated than that."

"We've just always felt tied together, the three of us. Even Rhydian, broody bastard that he is."

"It started in university," Finlay said. "We met and just... clicked. Like we were meant to find each other."

"But there was always something missing," Knox added, his usual playful look fading. "A hollowness, right here." He pressed his hand to his chest, just below his heart.

I gasped, my hand flying to my own chest. "You felt it too? That... ache?"

They both nodded, but didn't seem surprised that I understood.

"It's like a void," I whispered, pressing my palm against my sternum. "Right here, just left of centre. Like a piece of me was missing."

"Exactly," Finlay breathed. "That's exactly it."

"Being together helped," Knox said. "Made the ache less... well, achy. And sharing became a way to feel closer, more complete."

"It was never about the sex," Finlay added quickly. "Well, not entirely. It was about connection, about trying to fill that void."

I stared at the ceiling, stunned. "I thought I was the only one who felt that way. Like something was missing."

Knox leaned forward, his eyes intense. "And now? With us?"

I pursed my lips, turning my focus inward. "It's better," I said. "Still there, but... less."

Finlay nodded, a small smile playing on his lips. "That's how we feel too. Since you've been here, it's like..."

"Like puzzle pieces falling into place," Knox finished.

My brow furrowed even as misplaced hope unfurled in my chest. "What does it mean?"

Knox grinned, some of his usual swagger returning. "It means, Sparky, that you're stuck with us."

Finlay rolled his eyes at Knox but nodded in agreement. "We don't know exactly what this is, but we definitely want to see you beyond this weekend."

"What about Rhydian?" I asked hesitantly. "Doesn't it feel... incomplete without him here?"

Knox and Finlay exchanged a look, a flicker of something — pain? longing? — passing between them.

"Right now, it does," Finlay whispered. "But Rhydian's always been a part of us, even when he tries to keep his distance."

Knox nodded, his usual playful demeanour subdued. "The big lug thinks he's protecting us by staying away. But he's as much a part of this as we are."

"Will he come around?"

"Absolutely," Fin said, his tone harsh.

"He can't fight this forever." Knox smiled. "None of us can."

It was crazy, wasn't it? To feel so connected to people I barely knew? To contemplate diving into... whatever this was?

CHAPTER EIGHT

EDIN

*D*aylight forced its way beneath my exhausted eyelids far sooner than I'd have liked. I tried to resist waking, instead enjoying the quiet in my mind and my deliciously sore muscles.

But slowly, I became aware of the warm press of bodies on either side of me, the possessive drape of an arm across my bare stomach. For a disorienting moment, I couldn't place where I was or why everything felt so different...

Then it all came rushing back. Knox. Finlay. Our wild, passionate night together.

Holy hell.

A giddy laugh bubbled up inside me, escaping in an awed huff of air.

I'd really done it.

Thrown caution to the wind like Veronica demanded and leapt into the unknown with two men I barely knew but who made me feel more alive, more *seen*, than anyone else ever had.

I tensed for a split second, old habits threatening to rise up and send me bolting. But then Finlay nuzzled into the crook of my neck with a sleepy sigh and Knox's hand flexed against my stomach and I melted.

It felt right. Like I was exactly where I was meant to be, slotted between them as if I'd been carved to fit. My magic hummed beneath my skin, contented little sparks where before it had roiled and bucked against my control.

A pang of longing soured my contentment. Rhydian was the missing piece, the aching absence that kept this from feeling *completely* perfect. But I shoved the useless want aside. I had more than I'd ever dreamed of with just the two of them.

"Morning, beautiful," Knox said, his voice sleep-roughed but achingly tender. His lashes fluttered and he blinked at me, an awe-filled smile touching his lips. "You're a sight for sore eyes."

He rolled onto his back and stretched. Some of his joints clicked and popped painfully, but he didn't seem to mind.

I smirked. "Sore, huh?"

"The best kind." Satisfaction chased away the last of the cobwebs from his eyes. "Not sure if I dreamed you or if my imagination's just that good."

"Oh, I'm very real. Though I'm happy to remind you..."

A glint of heat sparked in his gaze, but then concern furrowed his brow. "How are you feeling? We weren't too... enthusiastic?"

Something incredibly soft unfurled beneath my ribs at his obvious care. I framed his face with my hands, drawing him close enough to taste my sincerity in a kiss.

"I feel amazing," I whispered against his lips. "You were both... incredible."

He rumbled in approval but the worry in his eyes didn't dim. "You'd tell us, if it was too much?"

My heart twisted, aching to smooth the vulnerability from his usually confident, cocky expression. "You could never be too much."

Gratitude, affection and something infinitely more fragile glimmered in the blue of his eyes before he claimed my mouth again, a wealth of emotion in the sweet slide of his lips over mine.

Eventually he pulled back with a shaky chuckle. "Keep kissing me like that and we'll wake up poor Fin."

He had crashed pretty hard last night — this morning?

I grinned. "Promises, promises."

He nipped playfully at my bottom lip before rolling out of bed in a mouthwatering display of muscle. "Don't you move, lass. I'm going to make you a feast fit for a queen."

With his body bare and filling my vision, my mind went straight to the gutter. I clenched my fists, resisting the urge to reach out and pull him back into bed.

If you want another round, you should probably eat something.

Muttering to myself about logic having no place

here, I gave in to the urge to stretch like a contented cat. My muscles loosened deliciously, tiny aches making themselves known in all the best ways.

If I let myself think too much, I'd freak out. I wasn't easygoing and spontaneous like Veronica. Everything had a place in my life, I lived for routine and the rules. My bosses once re-organised our office floor and it had thrown me off my game for a month.

I had always been the take it slow girl. Regular dates and all of our secrets on the table before I even thought about jumping into bed with a guy.

Only with them, the idea of seeing them beyond this weekend filled me with inexplicable happiness. They'd hinted at wanting it of course, but could I really dive into something so unconventional?

But hadn't I already taken the plunge?

Part of me wanted to leap at the chance. The connection I felt with them was unlike anything I'd ever experienced. But another part, the cautious, rule-following Edin, baulked at the idea.

What would people say? Witches didn't form harems, we were a monogamous race. And yet, the thought of never seeing them again after this weekend made my chest ache in a way I wasn't ready to examine too closely.

The contentment I experienced now was unlike anything I'd ever known. Maybe it was worth exploring further.

Finlay grumbled adorably in his sleep, drawing my attention to him. Smiling, I turned onto my side and gave myself permission to take it all in.

I couldn't even blame the alcohol.

No, pure desperation drove my actions last night and it seemed to have paid off. I pressed a hand to my chest and took a deep breath. Giddy happiness flooded me as my power flared but immediately settled like a contented cat.

Speaking of cats, Grimm was probably plotting my demise right about now. My familiar had a flair for the dramatic that rivalled any Shakespearean actor. The grumpy furball hated being left alone. Sure, he could feed himself — familiars aren't helpless — but that wouldn't stop him from throwing a fit. I could already picture coming home to find my sofa in tatters.

But you know what? Even Grimm's incoming *cat*-astrophe couldn't dim my good mood right now.

My gaze drifted to Finlay's sleeping face. I couldn't begin to understand how they'd known they could help me, but I'd be eternally grateful.

Thank you, I thought at him.

Unable to resist, I leaned over to press butterfly kisses to the freckles that dusted his shoulder. He grumbled and batted me away, a reluctant grin tugging at his lips.

"Just ten more minutes, you needy witch." Then he rolled over and buried his head beneath a pillow like that would stop me if I really wanted to go again.

Laughing, I slipped from the bed and made my way towards what I hoped was Knox's bathroom. The sound of a soft thump made me glance over my head to find Finlay staring at me. Smirking, I ignored him and continued with an extra sway to my hips because I could *feel* his hungry gaze following.

Goddess, I'd never felt so wanted. So powerful in my own skin.

The first spray of the shower pulled a moan from my throat, the heat soothing well-used muscles. I let my mind drift as I worked shampoo through my hair, memories of skilful hands and worshipping mouths swirling to the surface...

"Room in there for two, Firefly?"

I shivered at the tired smokiness of Finlay's brogue, turning to find him leaning against the doorframe with a crinkle-eyed grin.

"I suppose I could be persuaded..."

And then he was on me, crowding me against slick tiles, and I lost myself to sensation, to slippery caresses and gasping laughter and languid, coaxing touches that sparked wildfire in my veins.

❄

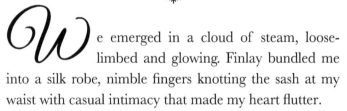

e emerged in a cloud of steam, loose-limbed and glowing. Finlay bundled me into a silk robe, nimble fingers knotting the sash at my waist with casual intimacy that made my heart flutter.

"There." He smoothed his hands over my shoulders, admiring his handiwork with a crooked grin. "All wrapped up like a present. Though I much prefer you in your birthday suit."

I laughed, sneaking a kiss to the corner of his

mouth. "Patience, my insatiable librarian. I'm saving the big reveal for after breakfast."

His eyes darkened, hands flexing on my hips. "Keep teasing me like that and we won't make it to the table."

"Oy! I can hear you two canoodling out there!" Knox's voice rang out from the kitchen, playfully aggrieved. "Stop hogging our woman and get your arses out here. Breakfast is served!"

Finlay rolled his eyes, fighting a smirk. "His Highness bellows."

"Can't have that pretty face of his getting all pouty, can we?" I walked my fingers up the centre of Finlay's chest, enjoying the way his breath stuttered. "After all, didn't your mother ever teach you to share?"

A wicked smile curved his mouth. "Oh, I'll share. Once I've had my fill..."

Heat licked through my veins at the intent smouldering behind his hazel eyes. I swayed into him, lips parting, a siren's call I was powerless to resist...

My stomach let out an awful sound, startling us both.

Finlay chuckled but took my hand and led me out of Knox's room, into the living space. We turned the corner and the mouthwatering scents wafting from the kitchen hit me.

Knox stood at the stove, his broad shoulders bare and muscles rippling as he flipped pancakes with expert ease. His hair was adorably mussed, and he hummed a tune I didn't recognise as he worked.

The sight of him so at home in the kitchen, wearing

nothing but low-slung sweatpants, stirred something warm in my chest. It was domestic and sexy all at once.

I perched on a stool at the breakfast bar, content to watch Knox move about with easy confidence, all dramatic flair and endearingly crooked grins shot over his shoulder.

"Special ingredient toast okay with you or should I whip up some chocolate strawberry crepes while the bacon crisps?"

I thought my eyes might actually roll back in my head. "That all sounds unreal."

"Got to keep my woman in fighting form," he winked, "if I'm to have any hope of keeping up."

I scoffed, cheeks pinking. "Flatterer."

"Truth-teller." He bopped me on the nose with a spatula, making me laugh.

As he slid a plate piled high with glistening bacon and golden toast in front of me, his lips brushed the shell of my ear. "Dig in, Sparky. Got to keep your strength up for later."

And didn't that just send a bolt of anticipation zipping down my spine...

I was so distracted by the promise in his eyes that I almost missed the bowl of berries Finlay set at my elbow. Popping a tart-sweet raspberry into my mouth, I hummed in bliss.

Knox groaned. "Christ, the sounds you make... Not sure if I'm jealous or inspired. Bet I could get you to be even louder..."

My pulse kicked into overdrive, body clenching as his fingertips trailed suggestively over my collarbone. I nipped at them when they ventured too close to my lips, revealing in his sharp inhale.

"Behave. We haven't even finished breakfast."

"Never let it be said I left my lass unsatisfied." His voice dipped into a register better suited for the bedroom. "In any… appetite."

And the worst part was, I believed him. Suspected he and Finlay would devote themselves to sating my every whim, if I let them. It was heady and terrifying and made me ache in places I didn't know I could feel.

Would Rhydian be just as devoted if he allowed himself to get close?

I plucked a strawberry from the bowl, stalling for nonchalance I definitely didn't feel. Knox's gaze locked onto the berry pressed to my bottom lip, colour riding high on his cheekbones.

Two could play at this game.

I bit into the fruit with deliberate slowness, hollowing my cheeks as I sucked at the tender flesh. He made a strangled sound as a trickle of juice escaped to run down my chin, eyes glittering with barely leashed want.

"Tease."

"Mmm, you love it." I swiped the juice away with my thumb, holding his gaze while I licked it clean.

The muscles in his throat worked as he swallowed convulsively. "Playing with fire."

I couldn't help my smirk. "Luckily for you, I'm something of an expert…"

A crack appeared in his composure, the wildfire behind it scorching through me. My magic leapt in response, embers stirring to life low in my belly. Not the destructive, terrifying heat I'd come to dread... but something infinitely headier.

"Where'd you learn to cook like this anyway?" I asked breathlessly, desperate for safer ground before I combusted on the spot. "You're like some kind of food wizard."

To my surprise, sadness cut through his expression before he blinked it away. "My mum taught me." He fiddled with a dishcloth, gaze faraway. "She had a bakery. Before the Council killed her."

My Council? "Why?"

I dreaded the answer and braced myself for reality to invade our peaceful bubble.

"She disagreed with them publicly," Knox said, his tone flat and his attention fixed on the crepes on the hot plate.

The Council, killing someone for disagreeing? That couldn't be right. The Council I knew was just and fair. They protected witches, they didn't harm them.

They were the guardians of our community, not... not murderers.

A memory flashed through my mind — hushed whispers in the office about a witch who'd been exiled. Dangerous magic, they'd said. A threat to everyone. I'd accepted it without question then, but now...

I shook my head, trying to dislodge the unsettling thoughts. There had to be more to Knox's story. There had to be.

I'd never heard of someone dying for disagreeing with the Witches Council.

But have you actually heard anyone disagree?

Well, no…

My stomach twisted. They knew I worked for the Council. How could they be so friendly with me, even want to pursue a relationship, knowing where my loyalties lay? Did Knox not realise the connection, or was there more to this than I understood?

"I'm so sorry," I said. "That must have been awful for you."

I wanted to ask more, to understand, but fear held me back.

"She sounds like she was an incredible woman," I managed around the lump in my throat. "You must miss her very much."

His smile wobbled precariously before he ducked his head, giving a jerky nod. "Every damn day."

The moment hung, intimate and raw, before he visibly gathered himself, a hint of mischief reappearing in his smile. "Come on then, tuck in. Can't have my food getting cold, it'd break my heart."

Doing as told, I settled back onto my stool and dug in again. As I ate, my mind whirled. Knox's story had shaken me more than I cared to admit. The Council I knew, the one I worked for, couldn't be capable of such cruelty. Could it?

But why would Knox lie?

The pain in his eyes had been real. I wavered, caught between the world I thought I knew and this new, unsettling possibility.

I glanced sidelong at Finlay. Butterflies took flight in my stomach when I found him already watching me, a softness in his gaze that hadn't been there before.

Like he was really seeing me, in a way no one else ever had.

"What's that big brain of yours chewing on?" I asked, nudging him with my elbow.

He startled, as if I'd pulled him from some deep reverie. A flush crept up his neck, pinking the tips of his ears in a way I found utterly endearing. "Ah, nothing much. Just… basking, I suppose."

There was a note of wonderment in his voice that set off a flutter low in my stomach. Like he couldn't quite believe his luck, couldn't fathom how he'd ended up here, with me.

That made two of us.

Before I could second-guess myself, I reached out to lace our fingers together, giving his hand a gentle squeeze. "I know the feeling."

His eyes met mine, a slow smile spreading across his face as his thumb traced maddening circles over my skin. It was such a simple touch, but it sent sparks skittering through my nerve endings. The same sparks I'd felt last night, when he and Knox had set me alight in ways I hadn't known were possible.

The memory alone was enough to make my blood sing. I'd never experienced anything like it — that sense of rightness, of completion. Like some essential piece of me I hadn't even known was missing had finally slotted into place.

It should have been terrifying. I barely knew them, these beautiful, mysterious men who'd upended my world in the span of a single night.

I wet my lips, struggling for nonchalance. "So,

what exactly does a sexy librarian like you do for fun, when you're not blowing innocent girls' minds?"

His answering grin turned positively wicked. Knox made a show of clearing his throat as he set a plate stacked high with glistening crepes before us. "Oy, stop trying to seduce our girl before she's even had her first cup of coffee. Poor form, mate."

Finlay rolled his eyes good-naturedly. "Like you're one to talk."

"I'll have you know I'm a perfect gentleman."

"A perfect gentleman who didn't let Edin come up for air the entire taxi ride here? Sure, keep telling yourself that..."

Their easy banter wrapped around me like a warm blanket. I could happily listen to them snark at each other for hours, revelling in the obvious affection beneath every playful jab.

It struck me then, how utterly at ease I felt wedged between them. Like I'd known them for years rather than hours. Even the ever-present knot of tension between my shoulder blades had unravelled, my body loose and relaxed in a way that had nothing to do with last night's activities.

And my magic...

As if conjured, a delicate flicker of heat stirred beneath my skin. Nothing like the roaring inferno that had raged out of control this past week, leaving smoking ruins in its wake. No, this was the gentle flame of a contented heart. Warm and grounding instead of wild and devastating.

It was everything I'd feared I'd lost. Everything I'd never dreamed I could have.

All because of two men I ran into at a bar.

If I believed in fate, I'd say it had orchestrated this moment. Pulled the strings of chance until they'd led me right to Knox and Finlay's door.

But that was crazy.

CHAPTER NINE

EDIN

*H*ours and many sessions in the bedroom later, we collapsed in the living room, all of our energy expended. I rested my head on a pillow in Finlay's lap while he read, his warmth seeping into my bones. His fingers danced along my arm, tracing nonsense patterns that somehow quieted the restless flickering of my magic.

It was strange how easily I fit here. Nestled against him. Like I'd always belonged in the negative space between them.

"Careful, Fin. Keep petting her like that and she'll start purring." Knox smirked at us from the armchair opposite.

Finlay's chuckle rumbled through me. "Aye, she's practically vibrating."

I flipped him a playful finger, too relaxed to find the

appropriate words. Besides, he wasn't wrong. Finlay's steady presence had my inner flames dimmed to a cosy simmer rather than their usual restless flickering. His quiet strength soothed me. It was so easy being here with them, like I'd found a home I never knew I was missing.

Part of me wished I could freeze this moment and live in it forever.

They fit into my life in ways I never expected.

Knox, with his easy confidence and playful charm, drew me out of my shell. His flirtatious quips and bold touches ignited something in me, a spark I didn't know I had. Yet he seemed to anticipate my needs before I even voiced them.

Finlay's quiet intensity balanced Knox's exuberance. His sharp mind and dry wit kept me on my toes, our conversations leaving me pleasantly buzzed. But it was the tender way he'd brush my hair back or squeeze my hand that truly melted my defences. His gentle nature soothed my frayed nerves when my thoughts threatened to spin out of control.

Between them both, I felt… different. Lighter, somehow. My magic, usually a restless force, purred contentedly in their presence. For the first time in ages, I felt at peace.

I couldn't explain it, but being with Knox and Finlay just felt right. Like I'd stumbled into something I didn't even know I was missing. It should have scared me, how quickly they'd become important to me.

Most people would kill to have what I had right here.

But there was still that lingering ache, that sense of something — someone — missing. Rhydian's brooding face flashed in my mind. The way he'd looked at me in that bar, all intensity and barely leashed power... I shivered.

What if choosing two over three fractured their decade-old bond? The last thing I wanted was to come between them.

I sighed, pushing the complicated thoughts aside. For now, I'd savour this perfect bubble with Knox and Finlay. Tomorrow could wait.

Finlay squinted at a battered paperback in his other hand, so deep in concentration that he barely noticed his reading glasses slipping down his nose.

Adorable. Utterly adorable.

"Nice glasses, Professor." I pushed them back into place for him with a tentative finger. I let a sultry note slide into my voice, just to see that hectic flush rise on his cheeks. "Very sexy librarian chic."

Finlay sputtered, his eyes widening behind the smudged lenses. "I was just... Um, I need them for reading sometimes."

Knox's cackle broke the intimate moment. "Smooth, Fin. Real smooth."

He reached for them, a blush staining his cheeks. I batted his hand away just like the cat they accused me of playing.

"Don't you dare take them off." I sat up and brushed a kiss across his lips. "I love seeing this side of you."

And I did. Fiercely, unexpectedly. These stolen

glimpses into the men beneath the magic, beneath the roles they donned like armour.

Finlay huffed a laugh against my mouth, the book forgotten as he tugged me closer. I let myself melt into him, into this pocket of peace we'd carved out just for a few days.

I wanted to learn them all, map every facet like my own personal atlas.

Including Rhydian?

The thought shattered my contented haze, a shard of sadness slivering through me. I chewed my lip, studying the dark hallway where he'd vanished last night. As if he couldn't bear to share space with me for more than a few charged minutes at a time.

Finlay caught my chin gently, forcing me to meet worried eyes, glasses gone and forgotten on the side table. "Hey. Where'd you go just now?"

I shrugged, offering a rueful quirk of my lips. A sad excuse for a smile, but all I could muster.

Apparently, I couldn't take my own advice and let it lie until tomorrow.

"Rhydian."

"Don't worry about tall, dark, and brooding." Knox leaned forward, his lips pursed while he searched for the right words. "He's just... adjusting. Not used to having someone new in his space, you know?"

But there was a tightness around his eyes, a smile that didn't quite reach the brilliant blue. And Finlay's fingers flexed against my skin, not quite a flinch but the ghost of one.

"He doesn't let people in easily," Finlay said.

My heart twisted. What kind of darkness had Rhydian tangled with to build those impenetrable walls?

A part of me — the reckless, curious part I usually kept locked away — itched to find out. Because, embarrassingly enough, I got it. Hadn't I done the same thing, just with a different mask? Throwing myself into work, clinging to routines like a lifeline, all to avoid confronting that yawning emptiness in my chest?

It was almost funny, in a sad sort of way. I was surrounded by literal magic, and yet I couldn't shake these all-too-human insecurities. But maybe that was the point. Maybe Rhydian and I weren't so different after all — just two people trying to keep our inner chaos in check.

Still I couldn't shake the feeling that there was more to Rhydian's story. And despite my better judgement, I wanted to know it.

"It's his loss," Knox said. "More Edin snuggles for us, eh Fin?"

Finlay snorted, the heavy moment broken. "Such a hardship."

They shrugged it off and I tried to go along with them. To smile and laugh and enjoy these stolen moments with them before our time ran out.

But no matter how I tried, I couldn't shake a strange need to have them all around me.

Suddenly restless, I hopped to my feet. "Right, I'm hungry. How about I whip up something for lunch? It's only fair after that incredible breakfast spread."

Knox raised a brow, a challenge glinting in his eyes.

"Oh? Think you can measure up to my culinary prowess, Sparky?"

I put my hands on my hips, matching his playful tone. "Excuse you, I'll have you know I make a mean grilled cheese. It's practically gourmet."

"Grilled cheese? Is that the best you've got?" Knox's grin widened. "And here I thought you might actually pose a challenge."

Rolling my eyes, I aimed a throw pillow at his head. "Oh, I'm sorry, not all of us can be master chefs. Some of us have other talents, you know."

He batted the pillow away, his amusement barely dented. "Do tell. What other talents are we talking about here?"

"Wouldn't you like to know." I smirked. "Now, are you going to let me near your precious kitchen, or are you too afraid I'll show you up?"

Knox chuckled, rising to his feet with a theatrical bow. "By all means, Sparky. The kitchen is yours. Dazzle us with your culinary masterpiece."

I paused at the Kitchen island, glancing back at Knox and Finlay. They were laughing about something, their eyes bright with amusement and affection. The sight made my heart clench with an emotion I wasn't ready to name.

My gaze drifted to the shadows in the corner of the room, half-expecting to see a pair of intense green eyes watching us. Would Rhydian ever join us like this, relaxed and open? Maybe if I cooked something he liked... But what would that even be? Brooding bastards and their mysterious tastes.

"Seriously though, I'm cooking. Any requests?" I called out, trying to keep my voice light despite the sudden tightness in my chest.

"Oh, we're being spoiled tonight!" Finlay clapped gleefully before affecting a snooty accent. "I'll have the lobster bisque and a nice Cab Sav, garçon."

"Hilarious." I shook my head. "Just for that, you might end up with burnt toast and a stern look."

Their mingled laughter chased me across the room. When was the last time I'd felt this... unburdened? This free from the weight of being the perfect, put-together Council secretary?

Too long. That's for sure. It felt like ages since I'd let myself relax like this. Before that nagging emptiness had set up shop in my chest and started gnawing away at me.

Until now. Until them.

What if I made enough for four? Would the smell of home-cooked food lure Rhydian out of whatever dark corner he was skulking in? It was worth a shot. After all, the way to a man's heart was through his stomach, right?

I smiled as I poked through the cabinets, assembling a collection of ingredients. Pasta, olive oil, a lonely onion. I could work with this. It wouldn't be gourmet, but it would be something. An offering and an olive branch all in one.

I let myself drift in the mindless rhythms of cooking, the sizzle of onions in the pan and the comforting glug of pasta water as it rolled to a boil. The clink of jars and utensils, the low simmer of the sauce as I coaxed it to life with a bit of this and that scavenged from the spice rack — it settled the jittery hum beneath my skin like nothing else could.

I was reaching for a dish towel, humming tunelessly under my breath, when a surge of heat, blistering and hungry, raced from my fingertips to ignite the fabric in a blink. Flames roared to eager life, devouring cotton and threading tongues of searing orange across the old linoleum counters without mercy.

I yelped, staggering back as panic clawed at my throat. Not here, not now. Not when I'd finally found a sliver of peace. Not when I thought we'd fixed it. Why hadn't we fixed it?

But my magic cared nothing for sentiment. It rebelled with vicious glee, sparks leaping from the counter to catch on cabinets, on curtains, on every scrap of fuel within reach. An inferno, birthed from my frustrating lack of control.

Dimly, I heard the shrill scream of the smoke detector, the clatter of footsteps pounding towards me. Finlay's voice rising in alarm, Knox's frantic shout of my name. But it all faded beneath the roar of my pulse in my ears, the relentless shriek of my magic as it strained against the tatters of my control.

I squeezed my eyes shut, willing the flames to obey. To subside, to gentle, to leash themselves once more. But they only climbed higher, hotter, whipped to frenzy by my terror.

Please, I begged, throat raw and eyes streaming from more than smoke. *Please, not like this, not here, I can't*—

"Enough."

A single word, cold as an arctic gale. It shuddered

through me, through the room, an impossible force. The very air stilled, the flames stuttering in confusion.

And then the shadows came.

They poured from every corner, every crevice, unfurling with liquid grace to envelop the space in icy darkness. The fire hissed and spat, fighting the loss of oxygen, but it was no use. The shadows swallowed the inferno whole, snuffing it out.

In the sudden, ringing silence, Rhydian's ragged breaths sounded like gunshots.

"Damn it, Edin!" he snarled, the shadows writhing around him in agitation. Poised to strike, to devour. "You're a Pyromancer, not a novice. How could you let it get this out of control?"

I flinched, stung by the accusation even as my body trembled in the aftermath of the blaze. "I don't know what's happening! My magic has never been this volatile before."

I stood behind the breakfast bar, surrounded by the chard, black destruction of their kitchen. If I weren't devastated, I'd laugh at the ridiculousness of my perfectly clean and clothed body and the circle of unmarked tile beneath my feet. Not even a speck of soot or ash settled on me.

But even as insane as it all seemed, I was grateful for the survival of the breakfast bar. It kept Rhydian and his furious expression away from me. His hands clenched at his side, like he desperately wanted to shake me. And who could blame him?

Maybe we should have spent the last twenty-four

hours actively working on my control instead of fucking each other on every available surface.

Finlay pushed past Rhydian, worry etched into every line of his face. He reached for me. "Edin, look at me. Breathe, love. It's okay, we're all safe."

But I stepped back, shame scalding through me hotter than any ember. The kitchen was a ruin of scorched wood and crumbling drywall, the acrid stench of smoke hanging thick and cloying.

"I'm sorry," I choked out, the words razors in my throat. "God, I'm so sorry. Your kitchen, I've ruined—"

"Hey, none of that." Knox's arm settled warm and heavy over my shoulders, solid and calming. "It's just stuff, it can be replaced."

"But she can't!" Rhydian whirled on Finlay and Knox, a vein jumping in his temple. "I thought you were supposed to be fixing this! Isn't that the whole point—?"

He cut himself off abruptly, gaze flicking to me and then away. As if I held the answer to some unspoken question, the key to a cipher only he knew.

Finlay frowned, head cocked. "We're trying. But this isn't exactly a situation that comes with a handbook. We're all flying blind here."

"Well, maybe if you'd stop pussyfooting around and actually tell her—"

"Tell me what?"

The silence stretched, taut and humming with tension. Knox scrubbed a hand over his face, looking suddenly exhausted. Finlay's fingers worried the cuff of his flannel, a nervous tic.

And Rhydian... Rhydian just watched me. Inscrutable and remote.

"It's complicated," Finlay said.

The word hung in the air, its bitter taste coating my tongue like ash. The same empty platitude I'd been force-fed my entire life, the same patronising dismissal that made my insides twist with frustration and disappointment.

You wouldn't understand, Edin. It's Council business, Edin. Just trust in the system, Edin. We know best.

"Complicated," I echoed, dully. "Right. Of course it is."

Knox's arm tightened around me. "What Fin means is... Look, Sparky. We're with you, okay? No matter how weird or scary or out of control this gets. We're not gonna bail just 'cause of a little magical hiccup."

Hiccup. As if I hadn't almost burned their home to cinders. As if I wasn't a livewire, a bomb primed to detonate at the slightest provocation. They should be running for the hills, not coddling me with sweet promises and gentle hands.

I shook my head, already retreating into myself. Into that numb, grey haze that had gotten me through so many Council meetings.

"You should," I whispered, the words scraping my throat raw. "You should run."

"Never," Knox said fiercely. He caught my chin with calloused fingers, forcing me to meet his gaze. Brilliant blue, luminous with conviction. "You're not getting rid of us that easily, Edin. We're in this for the long haul, unexpected fire and all."

I wanted to believe him. Wanted to burrow into the shelter of his arms, his certainty, and never surface. But hadn't I fallen for pretty lies before, chasing after acceptance, a place to belong?

My magic had always marked me as other. Too wild, too passionate, too much. A child of flame, destined to consume all she touched. And yet, with them... with Knox's determined spirit and Finlay's steady presence and the magnetic pull of Rhydian's shadows... I felt as if all my broken pieces had finally found their mates, slotting into place to form a mosaic of perfect imperfection.

So why was Rhydian pulling away? Why did he watch me with such pained longing only to retreat?

I opened my mouth, the questions battering at my teeth. Demanding release, resolution. But before I could give them voice, a glimmer caught my eye.

Three glimmering gold ropes stretched from my chest and into each of theirs. "Why is there a magical binding tying us together?"

I turned my head, assessing it from the corner of my eye. If I looked at them head-on, I couldn't see it. The reason I'd missed it all this time perhaps?

Finlay opened his mouth, a panicked glint in his eye and my expression hardened.

"And don't you dare tell me it's complicated," I said, my voice hard and unyielding.

CHAPTER TEN

"*W*ell?" Edin demanded, arms crossed tight over her chest.

I stared at her, the words I needed sticking in my throat. Her sad but frustrated gaze searched mine, boring into me as if she could scorch the truth from my very soul.

Goddess, where to even begin? How could I make her understand the sheer enormity of what bound us, the ancient threads of destiny that even I could barely comprehend?

"Edin, love, it's not what you think." I winced at the tremor in my voice. "Those threads, they represent a bond between us. A... a soulbond."

Her eyes widened, a spark of excitement flashing through them before dimming. "What does that mean?"

She glanced at the glimmering strands again and her

expression softened. I could practically see the gears turning behind her eyes, the conclusions she was leaping to without all the facts.

"Is this why I feel so... complete with you?" Her voice wavered, hope and hesitation intertwining. "Is this what you meant by 'helping' me?"

"Yes," I breathed, relief flooding through me. "Edin, I swear on my life, we didn't do this. It's a blessing from The Morrigan herself."

Her laugh was soft, tinged with awe. "The Morrigan? The goddess who abandoned Witchkind centuries ago? Why would she choose me... us?"

Knox stepped up beside me, his usual easy grin nowhere in sight. "We were just as surprised as you when the marks appeared."

I shot him a warning look, cursing internally. We hadn't even gotten to the serch bythol yet.

"What marks?" Edin's gaze darted between us, wild and cornered.

Without a word, Knox tugged the colour of his t-shirt down and tapped the swirling symbol above his heart. She'd traced it hundreds of times by now. "That's a soulbond mark?" I nodded and her eyes widened. "I just thought you'd all gotten the same tattoo."

Despite the flutter of anxiety in my chest, I smiled. "No, Firefly. Only Rhydian had tattoos before last week." I rubbed mine and winced remembering the pain of its branding. "We didn't know what this was before then either. I had to dig through the library archives to find so much as a mention of the brands. They're The Morrigan's mark. They signify that we've found the final piece of our soul, that we belong to you and you to us."

She tensed, her eyes darting to Rhydian. "I belong to no one but myself."

My heart clenched at the sadness in her tone, the resignation simmering beneath. Goddess, this was all wrong.

"Of course, love." Knox took another step forward, his flirty smile firmly in place. It couldn't hide the concern in his eyes though. "But it's also a physical mark of our compatibility, and one day, I hope, our love for one another. Bit more permanent and meaningful than a wedding ring don't you think?"

"Love? Wedding rings?" Her gaze raked across us all, lingering on Rhydian. "I've known you lot for a day! And now you're telling me some long-forgotten goddess has decided to play matchmaker?"

"In a manner of speaking."

She laughed, a hint of sadness in the sound. "It's incredible, but... I can't do this. Not when..." She glanced at Rhydian again.

I stepped forward, hands raised in supplication. Desperate to soothe, to explain. "Please, just listen—"

"Why didn't you tell me last night?" she asked quietly. "Before I... before we..."

I scrubbed a hand over my face, exhaustion and frustration warring in my veins. Why couldn't she see we were trying to protect her? That we'd only kept silent to avoid overwhelming her?

"We were going to tell you," I said quietly. Meeting her sad stare dead on, holding nothing back. "I swear it,

Edin. We just wanted to ease you into it, not drop this metaphysical bombshell on you all at once."

"I understand," she whispered. "But it doesn't change anything. I can't... I won't come between you all."

"Edin, please." I didn't bother hiding the naked emotion roughening my voice. "I know this is a lot. I know you're scared and confused but... we're here. We're with you, no matter what. If you'll just let me explain—"

"There's nothing to explain," she said, her voice thick with unshed tears. "I see how Rhydian looks at me. He doesn't want this... or me."

Rhydian, silent until now, let out a growl of pure frustration. "For fuck's sake, woman, we're trying to keep you *safe*!"

He slammed a fist against the burned wall, the shadows rippling in agitation. Mirroring the turmoil churning in my gut, the dread knotting my stomach. Drywall fell away, crashing to the scarred floor, but we ignored it.

"Do you have any idea the kind of danger you're in right now? What could happen if the wrong people found out about our connection?"

Edin rounded on him, tears glistening in her eyes. In that moment, she was every inch the council witch. Regal, implacable. Heartbroken.

"I can protect myself," she said softly. "Whatever this connection is, it's not worth tearing you all apart."

She marched toward the door, her shoulders set.

"Edin, wait!" I lunged after her, panic clawing at my

throat. Choking me. "You don't understand the risks. There are things out there, people who would use you to get to Rhydian. To us."

But she didn't even spare me a backward glance. Just wrenched the door open.

"I'm sorry," she said, refusing to turn around. "I can't be what you need me to be."

I recoiled as if she'd struck me.

"We can't let you go off half-cocked like this," Knox muttered, grim certainty lacing every word. "I've never put stock in Rhydian's enemies, but now with you in the picture, I can't disregard it. Edin, love, it's not safe for you out there."

"Please, don't make this harder than it already is," she pleaded, her voice breaking. "I'm a council witch. I can handle walking home alone in my own damn city."

The door slammed with a resounding finality, the walls shuddering in its wake.

Knox and I cursed, turning to Rhydian with desperate eyes.

"Tell her you want this too," Knox begged. "Tell her she's not coming between us!"

"She needs to hear it from you, Rhyd. We can't lose her like this."

But he remained silent, his face an unreadable mask as he stared at the closed door.

I'd always scoffed at his dark mutterings of vendettas and blood debts. The ever-present spectre of retribution stalking his steps, hungering for those he held dear. But with Edin, my Edin, out there alone and ignorant of the forces that would tear her apart to get to us… I believed.

Oh, I believed, with a soul-deep terror that eclipsed all reason.

I saw it in every scar that mapped Rhydian's skin, felt it in the haunted weight of his gaze when he thought we weren't looking. The blood on his hands, the enemies lurking in wait. Enemies that would stop at nothing to destroy anyone he cared about.

No matter how he protested, that small circle now included Edin... brave, beautiful Edin, with her heart of wildfire and will of steel.

But it was more than that. Until she accepted us and what the bond meant, her magic would continue to riot. She needed us, whether she wanted to admit it or not.

I didn't want to imagine what could happen to her without us. Refused to let my mind wander down those bleak paths, to envision her broken and lost. Consumed by the very power meant to sustain her.

Knox squeezed my shoulder, something bleak in his gaze. A shared dread, an unspoken vow.

"She'll be back," was all he said. As if saying it aloud could make it true, could summon her through sheer force of will.

The words rang hollow. Because what if she *didn't* come back? What if, in our fumbling attempts to shield her, to ease her into this new reality... we'd only driven her away?

Please, I sent the desperate thought into the ether. A prayer to The Morrigan. *Please, let her come back.*

CHAPTER ELEVEN

EDIN

How could they do this to me? I stumbled into my flat, my chest tight and aching. The silence hit me like a slap, a stark contrast to the warmth and laughter I'd grown used to at the guys' place in just a day.

Anger and sadness warred within me, each fighting for dominance. I was furious at Rhydian for denying me the very thing that made me feel whole, devastated that I couldn't have them all. The emotional whiplash left me reeling.

The Goddess had to be toying with me, to make separation hurt this much after just twenty-four hours in their company. I fought to hold back the flood of tears waiting to cripple me.

All my life, I'd scoffed at the idea of fate, of some grand cosmic plan. I made my own choices. The idea that I might be cosmically bound to three men, without my knowledge or consent, and I couldn't even have them... it made me want to scream. Or break something.

A harsh laugh bubbled up my throat. Goddess, I'd been so stupid. Thinking the connection between us, that bone-deep rightness, was natural. Just pheromones and compatibility.

But it was just another lie, wasn't it? Another choice ripped away from me by someone else's actions.

Anger surged through me, hot and electric. It crackled along my nerves, dancing at my fingertips. My magic roared to furious life in the palm of my hand. I clenched my fists, grinding my teeth against the temptation.

Control, Edin. Breathe.

But it was too late. A stray spark leapt from my skin, arcing through the air. It landed on my curtains, and the flimsy fabric went up like kindling.

"Shit!"

I lunged for the fire extinguisher, my brain a panicked buzz. Smoke stung my eyes as I doused the flames, the chemical stench coating my throat.

Finally, blessedly, the foam did its job and the fire died. I slumped against the wall, my knees giving way as I gasped for air. My eyes burned and my throat closed up as futile frustration overrode me and I lost control of the tears.

Goddess, what is happening to me?

My magic was a living thing inside me, feral and

ravenous with a mind of its own. It prowled beneath my skin, seeking escape. Seeking... something.

Someone, a voice whispered. *Three someones.*

"No!"

I dug the heels of my hands into my eyes. I wouldn't think about them. Not now, not yet. Not when the ache of their absence threatened to consume me.

"Well, well, well. Look what the cat dragged in."

I jumped at the sudden thick Scottish voice, my heart racing. Grimm, my familiar, sat on the kitchen counter, his tail swishing back and forth in agitation. His green eyes glowed with annoyance.

"Grimm," I sighed, "I'm really not in the mood for—"

"Not in the mood?" he hissed. "I've been worried sick! Two days, Edin. Two days without so much as a voicemail. What happened to 'I'll be back in a few hours'?"

I rolled my eyes, exasperation momentarily over-riding my emotional turmoil. "You hate having me around, and you can feed yourself. What's the big deal?"

Grimm's fur bristled. "Ye could have been dead in a ditch."

"I wasn't."

He glared at me from the counter. "How would I have known any differently? Ye don't disappear for days without warning."

I softened, moving closer to scratch behind his ears. "Were you actually worried about me, you old grump?"

"Don't push it," he grumbled, but he leaned into my

touch. "It's my job to look out for ye. Don't read any more into it."

A small smile tugged at my lips. "Aww, you do care."

"I said don't push it," he growled, but there was no real heat in it. "Just... don't do that again, aye? My nerves can't take it."

"Your nerves?" I laughed, feeling lighter than I had since leaving the guys' place. "You're practically ancient. I thought nothing could rattle you."

"Keep it up, and I'll cough up a hairball in yer shoes," Grimm said, but I could read the relief on his furry face.

For a moment, I let myself bask in the familiar banter, grateful for this bit of normalcy after the last week.

But reality crashed back in all too soon.

I needed answers. Needed to understand this thing inside me. But who could I ask? The council was a dead end. We didn't talk about gods. As far as they and every living witch was concerned, our power came from a well within the earth. It had nothing to do with the gods we apparently prayed to and worshipped at one point in our history.

Before meeting Knox, I would laugh at my sudden paranoia. Unfortunately, my brain now saw the pieces of the puzzle I'd always denied.

No. If I uttered the word Goddess to anyone within the Witches Council beyond an abstract affirmation of surprise, they'd take too much notice.

There had to be someone safer I could turn to.

Hamish.

I stopped pacing. My brother had spent most of our childhood spouting alternative theories. If anyone could make sense of this soulbond stuff, it was him.

But the thought of calling him, of bridging that gap... it sent ice water trickling down my spine. We hadn't spoken in four years. Not since I'd thrown his warnings about the council in his face.

They'll chew you up and spit you out, Edie, he'd said. *They destroy everything they touch.*

But I hadn't listened. I'd been so eager to belong, to have a purpose. I thought the council could give me that.

You should have listened.

And maybe I should have. Maybe Hamish had been right all along, with his conspiracy theories and dire predictions. With Knox's story ringing in my ears, the brutal murder of his mom, just for defying them...

If they could do that, what else were they capable of?

I chewed my lip, indecision churning in my gut. I'd sworn I'd never go crawling back to him. Not until he admitted he was wrong about me. But had he been? Or had I just been too blind to see it?

Still, this wasn't life or death. As much as I wanted answers, I couldn't bring myself to make that call. Not yet. The wound between us was still too raw, too deep.

"Fuck," I whispered, squeezing my eyes shut. "Fuck, fuck, fuck."

I felt cracked open, stripped bare. Everything I thought I knew, everything I thought I was... it was all unravelling, the threads slipping through my fingers faster than I could catch them.

And beneath it all, that hollow ache pulsed. The soulbond, tugging at me. Urging me back to the warmth and protection of my mates.

My mates. The words sent a shiver down my spine. Terrifying and thrilling in equal measure.

But I couldn't go back. Not yet. Not when Rhydian so clearly didn't want me. Not when the thought of being so close, yet so far from what I truly wanted threatened to tear me apart.

"What's wrong with ye?" Grimm asked, his tone dripping with sarcasm. "You look about as put together as a haggis after a caber toss."

I managed a weak smile. "I just... I need time to process everything."

Grimm narrowed his eyes, padding closer to me. He sniffed the air, his whiskers twitching. Suddenly, his eyes widened.

"Now that's a scent I haven't smelled in over three hundred years," he muttered, his Scottish brogue thickening.

"What are you talking about?" I asked, confusion momentarily overriding my emotional turmoil.

Grimm tilted his head, studying me. "I should've known when ye started setting the flat ablaze like a wee bairn with its first spark. But now that ye've begun to seal the bond... it's plain as day, lass."

My jaw dropped. "You know about the soulbond?"

"Of course I do, ye daft quine," he scoffed. "I've been around since before yer great-great-granny was a twinkle in her father's eye. I've seen a few in my time. Though I never thought I'd see one again, let alone be stuck with a witch dumb enough to run away from hers."

"I didn't run. I just... needed space to think. It's not every day you find out you're magically bound to three men you barely know." I paused, my voice dropping. "Besides, Rhydian made it clear he didn't want me. I wasn't about to drive a wedge between their friendship by choosing Knox and Finlay over him. That wouldn't have been fair to any of us."

Grimm's tail twitched, his expression softening slightly. "Matters of the heart are never straightforward, are they, lass?"

I sighed, running a hand through my hair. "No, they're not. But I came back, didn't I? That has to count for something."

"It does," Grimm said. "Though nearly burning yourself to a crisp was a bit dramatic, even for ye."

I winced, unable to argue with that. "Okay, so maybe I panicked a little. But can you blame me? This is all so... overwhelming."

"Overwhelming or not, running from a soulbond is like trying to outswim the tide. Futile and likely to get ye drowned."

I stared at Grimm. "How uh—" I cleared my throat, nervous energy trying to choke me. "What does it mean and why didn't you ever tell me about them?"

"Why would I tell ye? It's not exactly common knowledge these days, is it?"

I stared at him, unwilling to back down.

"Fine." He sighed. "The stories speak of an eternal, a gift from The Morrigan, goddess of witches. A way to mark those she'd favoured with soulmates and destined to fight by her side when the last days come."

Destined. Gifted. The words lodged in my throat, heavy as stones.

"Last days?"

"Of course, you don't know about prophecies." Grimm laughed, the sound bitter. "The council's done a bang-up job of erasing that bit of history."

"Why would they do that?"

"Why does any governing body do anything?" He shook his head at me, utter disappointment rolling through his aura. "Power, of course. Have I taught ye naught?"

For years, I'd dismissed his rants as the bitter ramblings of a criminal who couldn't accept his punishment. "I always thought you were just... I don't know, holding a grudge," I said, running a hand through my hair.

He grunted. "Aye, I suppose that's one way to put it. But tell me, lass, after all these years with me, do ye still think me nothing more than a disgruntled criminal?"

Knox's story about his mother's murder echoed inside my mind. A chill ran down my spine. "I... I don't know what to think anymore. Were they really that bad in your day?"

He let out a harsh laugh. "Bad? They were worse, if you can believe it. At least now they pretend to have some semblance of morality. Back then, they didn't even bother with the facade."

"And that's why they erased the knowledge of soul-bonds from Witchkind?"

"Aye. It's ancient magic, that." Grimm's tail twitched in agitation. "The council saw them as a threat to their power. Imagine, witches with amplified powers, connected on a level the Council couldnae control or manipulate. Of course they wanted to stamp it out."

I frowned, processing this. "But why me? Why now?"

"Who knows why the Goddess does anything?" he said, rolling his eyes. "But I'll tell ye this — in my day, a soulbond was considered a blessing. Witches would've given their right arm for what you have."

His words stung, reminding me of what I'd lost — or never really had. A stronger woman would be able to ignore the disinterest from someone who by all rights should be perfect for her. I'd always thought I was that person. I was fearless and stubborn to a fault, but I had never been selfish. And it would be selfish to drive a wedge between Knox, Finlay, and Rhydian.

"It doesn't feel like much of a blessing right now," I muttered.

Grimm's expression softened, just a fraction. "Ach, lass. I know it's scary. But ye can't let fear keep ye from something like this. Trust me, I've had centuries to learn that lesson."

I stared at Grimm, really considering his age for the first time. How many centuries had he seen? What secrets did he hold behind those glowing green eyes?

If the Council had lied about soulbonds and executing witches like Knox's mother for dissenting with them, what else had they lied about? How much of what I thought I knew was actually true?

I swallowed hard, steeling myself. "The Council told me you were a necromancer gone rogue. That you experimented with forbidden magic, threatening our entire society. They said your punishment was merciful, a chance at redemption." The words tasted bitter on my tongue. "But that's not true, is it?"

He fixed me with a level stare, his tail swishing slowly. "Depends on who ye ask, lass. To the Council, I *was* a traitor of the highest order. To others... Well, let's just say history is written by the victors."

I thought of Knox's story, of his mother murdered for speaking out. A chill ran down my spine. "What really happened? What did you do?"

Grimm was silent for a long moment, his gaze distant. When he spoke, his voice was low, tinged with an ancient sadness. "I tried to make our folk see what the Council was becoming. The power they were gathering, the liberties they were taking with our traditions, our very magic."

"And for that, they cursed you?" I asked, incredulous.

He let out a harsh laugh. "Oh no, lass. That was just the beginning. When warnings didn't work, I... took more drastic measures."

I leaned forward, hanging on his every word. "What kind of measures?"

"I led a rebellion," he said. "Joined and gathered like-minded witches, those who could see the corruption festering at the heart of the Council. We planned to overthrow them, to return power to the people."

My eyes widened. "What happened?"

Grimm's expression darkened. "We failed. The Council's reach was longer, their influence deeper than we'd anticipated. They crushed us, made examples of the leaders. And me? Well, they decided death was too good for me."

I swallowed hard, my throat suddenly dry. "So they cursed you to... this?"

He nodded. "Eternity as a cat, never dying, serving as a familiar to atone for my 'sins' against the Council. A fitting punishment, they thought, for one who dared to challenge their authority."

I sat back, stunned. All this time, I'd believed the Council's version of events and shrugged Grimm off as an ungrateful, grumpy old convict with a chip on his shoulder because he'd been caught. But this... this changed everything.

"I... I'm so sorry," I whispered.

He shook his head. "Don't be, lass. I made my choices, and I'd make them again. The question is, what will ye do with this knowledge?"

I bit my lip, uncertainty churning in my gut. "I don't know. It's all so much to take in."

Grimm's eyes softened. "Aye, it is. But you have a chance at something rare and precious. Even if one of yer mates is being a stubborn arse, ye need to fight for it."

I thought of Rhydian's rejection, the pain still fresh. "I don't know if I can," I whispered.

"Ye can, lass. Ye're stronger than ye know. Now, get some sleep. Things might look brighter in the morning."

As I headed to my bedroom, Grimm's voice stopped me. "And Edin? Remember — love, real love, is worth fighting for. Even if it scares the shite out of ye."

I shuffled to my bedroom, my body heavy as a stone and my mind a swirling pit of contradicting thoughts and feelings that I had no hope of deciphering. Not tonight anyway. The sheets were cold against my skin. Too empty, too quiet. My magic hummed beneath my skin, restless and searching. It pulled at my core, urging me to go back to them.

But I couldn't.

So I lay there, tears leaking down my cheeks. Aching for three bodies beside me, for the scent of sandalwood and cloves. Torn between the anger at being denied what I so desperately wanted and the soul-deep sadness of separation. The revelation about the Council's true nature only added to my turmoil.

Tomorrow. I'd figure it out tomorrow.

For now, I'd try to sleep, and hope that morning would bring some clarity to this mess. And maybe, just maybe, I'd gather the courage to face my bond mates again — and to start questioning everything I thought I knew about the Witches Council.

CHAPTER TWELVE

EDIN

I tossed and turned, my mind spinning with everything Grimm had said. The ache of being away from my soulmates gnawed at me, making sleep impossible.

Soulmates. The word still made me shiver, excited and scared all at once.

It didn't make sense. That some cosmic power had looked at my broken pieces and seen how I could fit with three others... It went against everything I'd ever believed.

But I couldn't ignore how right it felt. How my magic calmed with them, how they filled up the empty spaces in me. Like I'd been waiting for them my whole life without knowing.

And now, to have that ripped away because Rhydian didn't want me... it was unbearable.

I groaned, covering my eyes. I was a total mess. Wanting them so bad it hurt, but knowing I couldn't have them all. I couldn't drive a wedge between Knox, Finlay, and Rhydian. Who was I to come between them? And now, with everything I'd learned about the Council... My entire world was crumbling. Nothing was as it seemed.

The scent of smoke hit me and my eyes flew open, my heart racing. The pillow beside me was on fire, flames licking hungrily at the fabric.

"No," I cried, the sound barely audible as the word smoke and despair choked me. Would it never end?

"Oi! Watch where yer flinging that fire, ye daft quine!" Grimm yowled, leaping from his warm spot near my head. He landed on the floor with an indignant huff, fur standing on end. "I was having a perfectly good kip, and ye had to go and ruin it with yer fire-spitting shenanigans!"

I bolted upright, hands shaking as I tried to smother the blaze. But the flames just got bigger, burning my hands. Panic clawed at my throat. My magic surged under my skin.

"Stop," I begged, my voice breaking. "Please, stop!"

But it was like my magic couldn't hear me. Like it wanted to burn me up from the inside.

Coughing on smoke, I stumbled out of bed and grabbed the fire extinguisher yet again. Sleeping was clearly too dangerous when my control was shot to hell from being away from *them*.

After dousing my bed in foam, I stumbled into the living room, far more awake than I'd have liked for 1

AM. I hugged myself, trying to keep my magic in check.

But how trust myself, when I felt ripped open and raw? I couldn't even trust my own magic or the institution I'd dedicated my life to. The Council, with its lies and manipulations...

I paced, sparks trailing behind me, scorching the floor. The air felt thick and heavy with heat. My heart ached, thinking of Knox and Finlay, of the connection we'd shared. And Rhydian... his rejection stung sharply, a constant throb in my chest.

It all twisted together — the bond, the Council's deception, Rhydian's rejection — a knot of pain and confusion in my gut.

"You're stronger than this." But the words rang hollow.

I wasn't strong. I was weak, so damn weak. Worn down from fighting and worrying about my magic control for a week. Hollowed out by the bond pulling at me, screaming for my soulmates. Shattered by the realisation that the Council, my beacon of truth and justice, was built on lies. I was unravelling at the seams, a live wire spitting sparks.

And under it all, that emptiness pulsed. The hole in my chest where Knox, Finlay and Rhydian should be. Even if I could never truly have them all.

It was too much. Too big, too raw. A tidal wave battering at my ribcage. I couldn't hold it, couldn't contain it.

With a sob, I fell to my knees. And my magic exploded out of me in a storm of fire.

The world dissolved into heat and chaos. Fire roared up the walls, devouring curtains and furniture with greedy hunger. Smoke choked the air, thick and cloying. It seared my lungs, blinded me with tears.

"Grimm! Where are you?"

I couldn't see him through the inferno, but I heard his yowl of alarm.

"No," I coughed, scrabbling backwards on my hands and knees. "No, please, I don't want this!"

But my magic was rabid, an inferno with a mind of its own. It consumed everything it touched, not caring how I begged. Somehow, miraculously, the flames seemed to part around him, never quite touching his fur.

I reached for the flames with my power, trying to smother them. But it was like grasping at quicksilver - the fire only roared higher, feeding on my fear. The heat was unbearable. It battered my skin, raining blistering embers in my hair, my clothes. The smoke was blinding, suffocating.

I couldn't breathe. Couldn't see. My control shattered. This was it. I was going to die, eaten up by my own magic.

My strength gave out and I fell, coughing and choking. Bitter regret filled my mouth.

Darkness crept in, threaded with flame. This was the end. My magic would swallow me whole, leaving nothing but ashes.

"Edin!" Rhydian shouted, his voice hoarse and almost lost in the crackling fire. "Take my hand, now!"

I squinted at the hand hovering before me, barely believing it real.

Then he grabbed me, pulling me from the floor with a very real, very solid touch. A sob of relief escaped me as I lunged for him.

"Wait!" I choked out. I broke out of his grip and turned back towards the inferno. "Grimm! Where are you?"

Rhydian cursed. "We don't have time for this."

"I don't care." No way in hell would I leave my familiar here.

Thankfully, I'd barely taken a step when Grimm appeared from the smoke and leapt into my arms. Only then did I lunge for Rhydian, clutching the cat to my chest.

He wrapped his arms around me and sheltered me against his body.

"How did you know?" I choked out, my voice rough.

He didn't answer. Instead, the shadows surged around us, wiping out his grim expression and my view of the destruction. They wrapped around us, shielding us from the flames, tugging us into some in-between place where silence and darkness reigned.

I blinked and the crispness of Edinburgh at night hit me. We emerged on the pavement across the street from my tenement building beneath a blown out street light. Sirens wailed in the distance, but they were too far away to stop the fire claiming the building. The flames blew out my living room window before consuming the roof. Soon they'd take the entire block.

"We need to go, star."

I tore my gaze from the chaos of my street and the roaring of my emotions. Guilt and terror threatened to consume me. I focused on him, his wild green eyes in his ash-smeared face, his shaking hands on my shoulders.

"You came," I croaked, stuck on the only thing that mattered. "You saved me."

"I'll always find you," he said, raw and intense. "But this can't happen again. You *need* us, Edin. You have to accept the bond, or your magic will destroy you."

My heart clenched. "But... but you don't want me," I whispered, the words catching in my throat. "I can't come between you three. I won't be selfish like that."

"What in the blazes are ye on about?" Grimm interrupted, his Scottish brogue thick with irritation. "Of course he wants ye, ye daft bampot. They all do. It's a soulbond, for the love of the Goddess!"

Rhydian stiffened, his jaw clenching. "I'm my own person. No Goddess pulls my strings."

My heart sank at his words, but Grimm just snorted. "Aye, and I'm the Queen of England."

"Shh!" Rhydian hissed, glancing around. "We're in enough trouble without some human getting video of a talking cat."

Grimm bristled but fell silent, glaring at us both.

People poured out the front door, crying and coughing as the top floors blazed. Guilt twisted sharp in my gut.

"Oh Goddess." Fresh tears spilled down my cheeks. "Those people... I could've killed someone... how do I explain this to the Council, to work, I don't even know what I've *done*..."

"Shh, love, breathe." Rhydian cupped my face, tipping my chin up to meet his calm, determined gaze.

"We'll figure it out. But we need to go now. It isn't safe for you here."

"But I'll need to give a statement to the Witch patrol."

"No!" The word fell from his lips with the crack of a whip. "Waiting for the Witches Council's minions will only hurt you more."

"He's right," Grimm muttered, low enough that only we could hear. "If they find out about the soulbond... Well, let's just say it won't end well for any of us."

Fear gripped me, cold and sharp. "What would they do?"

"Nothing good," Rhydian said grimly. "Which is why we need to leave. Now."

How had it all gone so wrong? How had my life crumbled in days?

But I knew the answer, even as I shied away from it. I'd left my soulmates, thinking I was doing the right thing. I couldn't bear Rhydian's rejection or the thought of causing a rift between them. But I hadn't understood the true nature of the bond, the depth of what we were to each other. And in my ignorance, I'd thrown myself into free fall with no safety net to catch me.

Never again. I wouldn't make the same mistake twice.

"Okay," I whispered, fingers fisting in Rhydian's jacket. "Okay. Get me out of here. Please."

His eyes flashed, something fierce and possessive and achingly grateful. Then he scooped me up like I weighed nothing, holding me against his solid chest.

Grimm leaped onto his shoulder, clinging with extended claws.

As the shadows rose again, I let my eyes close. Let myself sink into the calm of his hold, his heartbeat calming my racing pulse. In a world where nothing was as it seemed — where the Council was corrupt and my own magic rebelled — at least this felt real.

I'd been an idiot to leave. To think I could protect them from myself, from the complications I brought. But no more. No more misunderstandings, no more hiding from the truth of what we were to each other.

No more blind faith in institutions or people that didn't deserve it.

Nothing more than ashes might have remained of my life, but one thing was crystal clear in all the chaos: I needed them more than I knew.

CHAPTER THIRTEEN

RHYDIAN

I stepped out of the shadows into our living room, Edin's trembling form cradled against my chest. The pungent scent of smoke clung to us. Even the edges of her pyjamas were singed. A stark reminder of how close I'd come to losing her. My heart hammered against my ribs, a mix of relief and lingering terror.

Grimm leaped from my shoulder with an indignant yowl. "Blasted shadows," he grumbled, shaking himself vigorously. "I hate travelling that way. It's like swimming through treacle."

"Next time I'll leave you there," I snapped, my nerves still raw.

Edin stirred weakly in my arms. "No," she protested, her voice weak "Don't..."

"Shh, it's alright," I murmured, softening my tone. "I'd never actually leave him behind."

Knox and Finlay burst into the room, their faces pale with worry.

"What happened?" Knox demanded, his usually cocky demeanour cracking. "Is she-—"

"Fire," I bit out, my voice rough. "Her magic got out of control again. Nearly burned down her entire building."

I gently set Edin down on the sofa, my hands lingering for a heartbeat too long. She looked so small, so fragile, curled in on herself with soot streaking her pale skin. My shadows writhed beneath my skin, desperate to wrap around her, to shield her from the world.

Get a grip. You can't protect her. You'll only make things worse.

Knox darted to the charred remains of our kitchen, returning with a glass of water and a damp cloth. Finlay sank down beside Edin, murmuring soothing nonsense as he rubbed circles on her back. I knelt before her, taking her trembling hands in mine before I could think better of it. They were ice-cold despite the inferno she'd just escaped.

"I'm sorry," I said, the words scraping my throat raw. "I should've gotten there faster."

Edin's amber eyes, still glazed with shock, met mine. "How... how did you know?" she whispered. "That I was in trouble?"

I stiffened, uncomfortable with the naked vulnerability in her gaze. "I felt it," I admitted grudgingly. "Through the bond."

A flicker of something — hope? relief? — crossed her face before she schooled her features.

"I'm grateful," she murmured. "For the bond. For you saving me. But I won't... I promise I won't read anything into it."

My chest constricted, an ache blooming beneath my sternum. I wanted to tell her she *should* read into it. That I'd move heaven and earth to keep her safe. That the thought of losing her before I'd even had her tore me apart.

But the words stuck in my throat, choking me with their impossibility.

"I should go," Edin continued, her voice small and defeated. "As soon as I stop shaking. Find a hotel or... something." She let out a hollow laugh. "Though I don't know how. Everything's gone. My phone, my cards... all of it, up in flames."

"No." Knox's voice cracked like a whip. He crouched beside me, his blue eyes blazing. "You're not going anywhere, Sparky. We'll do anything to keep you safe. Anything to make you happy."

Finlay nodded emphatically. "Please, stay. Let us help you."

I should've been relieved. They could take care of her, keep her close and protected while I... what? Ran away like a coward?

But jealousy, sharp and poisonous, flooded my veins. The thought of Knox and Finlay comforting her,

touching her, loving her while I skulked in the shadows...
it was almost more than I could bear.

"Well, isn't this a cosy little drama?" Grimm's
sardonic meow cut through the tension. "And here I
thought I'd seen it all in my three-hundred-and-seventy-
five years."

I retreated a step, shadows curling around my fingertips. The urge to protect her warred with the knowledge
of the danger I posed. My involvement in her life had
already nearly gotten her killed once. How many more
times would she suffer because of me?

I shot the cat a withering glare, but he just blinked
lazily at me from his perch on the coffee table. Smug
bastard.

"You're welcome to stay here as long as you need," I
heard myself say, the words distant and hollow. "You'll
be safe with Knox and Finlay."

Edin's gaze snapped to mine, hurt and confusion
warring in those amber depths. "And you?" she asked
softly. "Will you... will you stay too?"

I retreated a step, then another. "I need some air," I
muttered.

Grimm materialised beside me, tail swishing in irritation. "Whatever stupid shite yer're thinking," he
growled, "get over yerself. Soulbonds aren't so easily
shaken."

His words hit me like a physical blow. I turned away,
unable to face the truth in them. The shadows beckoned, offering escape from the suffocating weight of
emotion in the room.

I glowered at him. "Watch me," I bit out.

But even as the words left my mouth, I knew they were a lie. The bond thrummed between us, a living thing. It sang in my blood, whispering of belonging and completion. Of a future I'd never dared to imagine.

And that's exactly why I had to leave.

Ignoring Knox and Finlay's protests, the wounded look on Edin's face, I slipped into the comforting embrace of darkness. I didn't go far — just to the far corner of the living room, cloaked in shadow. Close enough to protect if needed, but hidden from view.

I watched as Knox fussed over Edin, bringing her more water and a blanket. As Finlay held her hand, speaking in low, soothing tones. They were good for her. Kind and open in all the ways I could never be.

She deserved their light, not my darkness.

The decision crystallised in my mind, as painful as it was inevitable. I would leave. For their safety, for Edin's happiness. It was the only way.

But as I steeled myself to slip away, to fade into the night and never look back, Edin's gaze found mine unerringly. Even cloaked in shadow, she saw me. And the naked longing in her eyes shattered something deep inside me.

Fuck.

I was so screwed.

CHAPTER FOURTEEN

FINLAY

"Damn it, Rhydian!" Knox exploded, his voice cutting through the stunned silence left in the wake of Rhydian's abrupt departure. "Stop running away like a bloody coward!"

My gaze fixed on the spot where Rhydian had vanished. The shadows in the corner still rippled faintly.

"He'll be back," I said, but the words rang hollow even to my own ears. "He always comes back."

Knox snorted, his arm tightening around Edin's shoulders where we sat huddled on the sofa. "Yeah, after he's done brooding and feeling sorry for himself. Meanwhile, we're left to deal with the fallout."

My gaze drifted to Edin, sandwiched between us. She looked so small, so vulnerable, wrapped in the blanket Knox had draped over her shoulders. Soot still smudged her pale skin, and her eyes were wide with shock and confusion. Guilt twisted in my gut, sharp and bitter.

This was our fault. My fault. If we'd just told her the truth from the beginning...

"I'm so sorry," I said, my voice cracking. I shifted to face her more fully, my hand finding hers where it rested on her lap. "If I'd told you about the soulbond sooner, maybe none of this would have happened."

She blinked, focusing on me with effort. "What?"

"The soulbond," I repeated, the words tumbling out in a desperate rush. "We should have explained everything right away. About The Morrigan, about the marks, about what it all means. But we were afraid of scaring you off, and then things got so complicated so quickly, and—"

"Finlay." Edin's fingers tightened around mine, stopping my rambling. Her touch was cool, grounding. "It's not your fault."

I shook my head, unable to accept her forgiveness. "But if we'd just been honest—"

"I probably wouldn't have believed you if you'd told me outright," she said, a wry smile tugging at her lips. "I mean, think about it. If you'd walked up to me in that bar and said, 'Hey, we're soulmates bound by an ancient goddess,' I'd have run screaming in the opposite direction."

A chuckle escaped me, surprising us both. "When you put it that way..."

"I needed to experience this connection for myself." Her thumb traced soothing circles on the back of my hand. "To feel it. And even then, I tried to run away."

"But we pushed you away," Knox said, his voice softer now. "We kept secrets, and Rhydian..." He trailed off, jaw clenching.

"Rhydian was being Rhydian," I finished for him. "Broody and noble and utterly infuriating."

Edin's lips quirked in a sad smile. "He's scared," she said softly. "I can feel it, through the bond. He's terrified of hurting us, of dragging us into whatever trouble he's wrapped himself in."

I nodded, a lump forming in my throat. Of course she could sense it. The bond thrummed between us all, a living, breathing thing. Even now, with Rhydian gone, I could feel the faint echo of his presence, like a phantom limb.

"That doesn't excuse him abandoning us," Knox growled, but some of the fight had gone out of him. He slumped back against the sofa, his free hand running through his tousled blond hair.

"No. It doesn't." Edin fidgeted with the edge of the blanket, her fingers tracing the soft fabric. "But I understand it. I tried to do the same thing, remember? I thought I was protecting you all by leaving."

I shuddered at the memory of that night, of the aching emptiness when she'd walked out our door. "And look how well that turned out," I muttered.

The black cat, who had been suspiciously quiet until now, let out a derisive snort from his perch on the coffee table. "Och, spare me the sappy reconciliation," he drawled, stretching languidly. "Yer're all idiots, if ye ask me. Soulbonds are rare and precious things. Ye don't run from them, ye embrace them with both hands and hold on for dear life."

I blinked, my mind reeling. A talking cat? No, not just a cat — a familiar. Edin had a familiar.

"You never told us you had a familiar," I said slowly, trying to keep my voice steady.

She looked sheepish, her gaze darting between me and the cat. "I... it never came up?"

Grimm snorted again. "Aye, because one simply forgets to mention their centuries-old, Council-cursed companion. How terribly forgetful of ye, dearie."

My eyebrows shot up. Council-cursed? This grumpy, sardonic cat was a victim of the Witches Council? The same council Edin worked for? My mind raced, connecting dots I hadn't even known existed.

"Hold on." Knox reared back, studying the cat with just as much bewilderment as I felt. "Can we back up a bit? Who — or what — exactly are you?"

The cat fixed Knox with a look that could only be described as condescending. "I, ye overgrown puppy, am Grimm Brodie. Edin's familiar, former rebel against the Witches Council. And ye lot are giving me a sore head with all this drama."

I couldn't help but chuckle, despite the seriousness of the situation. There was something oddly endearing about this cranky cat. But more importantly, his presence raised a host of new questions. I leaned forward, my scholarly curiosity piqued despite the emotional turmoil of the night.

"How long have you been with Edin? And what exactly did you do to anger the Council?"

Grimm's tail swished lazily. "Longer than she's been alive, laddie. As for the Council..." His green eyes narrowed. "Let's just say I had some disagreements with their methods. Nasty bunch, they are."

I glanced at Edin, who was chewing her lip nervously. "But you work for the Council," I said softly. "How does that...?"

"She doesn't know," Grimm interrupted. "Or didn't, until recently. The Council's quite good at keeping their darker deeds under wraps."

Knox whistled low. "Don't I know it."

I blinked in surprise, trying to process this new information. "Wait, so the Council gave you Grimm? But they don't approve of familiars."

Edin nodded, looking a bit sheepish. "Yeah, it's... complicated. They assigned him to me about a year after I started working there. Said it was standard procedure for all employees."

"So they use familiars to strengthen their witches, but claim they're dangerous while also using them as spies to keep tabs on their employees? That doesn't add up." I frowned, pieces starting to click into place. "Why would the Council need reports on their own employees in the first place? If everything was above board, there'd be no need for that level of surveillance."

Knox nodded in agreement. "Seems a bit shady if you ask me. What are they so afraid of?"

"I'd say they wanted to keep tabs on their wee pawns," Grimm said.

"So you falsified your reports to the Council?"

"Of course I did," Grimm huffed, looking

offended at the very suggestion he'd do otherwise. "What kind of familiar would I be if I didnae protect ma witch?"

The corner of Edin's lips curled up and she reached out, scratching behind Grimm's ear. "I love you too, you grumpy furball."

The cat spluttered. "I wouldn't go that far."

I leaned back, my mind whirling with this new information. "But why? What could they possibly gain from spying on their own people?"

Edin shifted uncomfortably between us. "I never really questioned it. But now..." She trailed off, biting her lip.

My heart ached for her. How long had she been kept in the dark, manipulated by the very organisation she trusted?

"Now you're wondering what else they might be lying about," I finished for her.

She nodded, looking troubled. "Exactly. What else have they hidden? And why?"

Grimm stretched lazily, but his eyes were sharp. "Och kitten, ye have nae idea how deep this rabbit hole goes. The Council's been playing a long game, and we're all just pieces on their chessboard."

A chill ran down my spine. What had we stumbled into? And more importantly, how were we going to keep Edin safe in the middle of it all?

"We need Rhydian," I said, the words slipping out before I could stop them. "He knows more about the Council's shadier dealings than any of us."

Knox nodded, his expression grim. "Yeah, but good

luck getting him to open up about it. He's more closed off than a bloody fortress."

Edin's breath hitched at the mention of Rhydian's name. "Do you think he'll come back?"

I opened my mouth to reassure her, but before I could speak, a flicker of flame caught my eye. A stack of papers on the coffee table, right next to Grimm, had begun to smoulder.

"Bleeding hell!" Grimm yowled, leaping away from the sudden fire. "Are ye trying to kill me, ye ungrateful witch? I swear, I'm too old for this nonsense!"

The cat darted out of the room, still shouting about the perils of soulbonds and fire-happy witches.

Knox sprang into action, grabbing a throw cushion and using it to smother the flames. "Easy, Sparky," he said, his tone gentle despite the urgency of his movements. "Deep breaths, yeah?"

Her eyes were wide with panic, her hands shaking as she stared at the smoking pile of papers. "I'm sorry, I didn't mean to — I can't control it—"

Before I could think better of it, I cupped her face in my hands and kissed her. It wasn't graceful or romantic — just a desperate press of lips, an attempt to ground her, soothe her magic while also reminding her she wasn't alone in this.

When I pulled back, Edin blinked at me, surprise written across her features. "What was that for?"

Heat crept up my neck. "Sorry, I just — you needed a distraction, and I thought—"

"It's okay," she said softly, a small smile playing at the corners of her mouth. "It helped, actually."

Knox flopped back onto the sofa, the crisis averted for now. "Well, that's one way to put out a fire." He chuckled.

Edin's smile faded, replaced by a look of grim determination. "I can't keep doing this," she said, gesturing to the charred remains of our paperwork. "I'm a danger to everyone around me."

"Hey, no." I took her hand in mine. "We'll figure this out. We'll help you get control."

"He's right." Knox slid his arm around her shoulders. "We've got you."

She stared between us, her eyes shining with unshed tears. "I think I need to stay here. At least until I can get a handle on my magic. It's not safe for me to be on my own right now."

Relief washed over me. "Yes," I breathed. "Please. Stay as long as you need."

Knox nodded enthusiastically. "What he said. Our home is your home, Sparky."

Her shoulders relaxed, some of the tension draining out of her. "Thank you," she whispered. "For everything."

CHAPTER FIFTEEN

EDIN

"What about this one, Firefly? Rhydian wouldn't be able to keep his hands off you."

I stood in the bustling department store, surrounded by racks of clothes and the low hum of shoppers' chatter. Finlay held up a scandalously short red dress, his eyes twinkling with cheekiness.

Heat rushed to my cheeks. "I need practical clothes, not... that."

He laughed, the sound warm and rich. "Come on, live a little. You can't tell me you haven't thought about it."

I snatched the dress from his hands, trying to ignore the way my heart raced at the thought of Rhydian's intense green eyes roving over me in this outfit. "I'll try it on, but only to prove how ridiculous it is."

Finlay's grin widened. "Sure, sure. Whatever you say."

My mind wandered while I made my way to the changing rooms, arms laden with a mix of sensible blouses and Finlay's more daring selections. It had only been a day since the fire, since I'd moved in with the guys, and everything still felt surreal. The soulbond hummed beneath my skin, a constant reminder of the new life I'd stumbled into.

I slipped into a changing cubicle, hanging the clothes on the hooks provided. My fingers lingered on the red dress, the silky fabric cool against my skin.

What would it be like to be wanted by all three of them? To belong, truly belong, to Rhydian, Knox, and Finlay?

The thought of it made me feel alive, more awake and seen than I had ever been. I'd spent so long feeling hollow, and now...

I shook my head, trying to clear the distracting thoughts. *You're here for clothes, not daydreams about your soulmates.*

I had just started to unbutton the white shirt I'd borrowed from Knox when a flicker of movement caught my eye in the mirror. Before I could turn, a hand clamped over my mouth, rough fabric scratching against my lips. The sickly sweet scent of chemicals filled my nose.

Panic exploded in my chest. I thrashed wildly, trying to scream, to summon my fire, anything. But my limbs felt heavy, uncoordinated. The world tilted sideways, darkness creeping in at the edges of my vision.

The last thing I saw was a pair of cold, grey eyes behind a black mask.

Then, nothing.

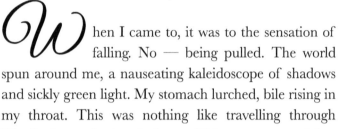

When I came to, it was to the sensation of falling. No — being pulled. The world spun around me, a nauseating kaleidoscope of shadows and sickly green light. My stomach lurched, bile rising in my throat. This was nothing like travelling through Rhydian's comforting darkness. This was wrong, violating, like being yanked through the cold void between worlds.

We burst out of the portal with a sickening lurch, and I stumbled, my knees hitting hard stone. The impact jolted through me, setting off explosions of pain behind my eyes. I retched, but nothing came up.

"Up you get, witch." A rough hand hauled me to my feet, shoving me into a chair. Cold metal bit into my wrists as manacles snapped shut, chaining me in place.

I blinked furiously, trying to clear my vision. Gradually, the world came into focus. I was in some kind of underground chamber, the walls slick with moisture and gleaming faintly in the dim light of flickering torches. The air was heavy with the musty scent of earth and decay.

I'd been here before, years ago when I first moved to Edinburgh. This was one of the Vaults, an eerie network of chambers beneath the city where prisoners were once kept. I remembered the ghost tour vividly — the guide's dramatic tales of torture and restless spirits, how I'd spent every moment desperate to get out and away from the claustrophobic feeling of invisible eyes on me.

But this was no tourist attraction now. The torches cast dancing shadows across rough stone walls, illuminating rusted chains that hung from iron rings set into the rock. My stomach churned as I imagined the suffering these walls had witnessed.

"Where—" My voice came out as a croak. I swallowed hard and tried again. "Where am I? What do you want?"

A chuckle echoed through the chamber, sending chills down my spine. "Oh, I think you know exactly why you're here."

A figure stepped out of the shadows — tall, imposing, clad in dark robes that seemed to drink in what little light there was. The Witches Council insignia glinted on his chest.

My blood froze as recognition hit me. Those piercing blue eyes, always accompanied by hushed whispers and sudden silences in the Council offices, now gleamed cold and predatory.

My muscles tensed, heart hammering against my ribs. I'd seen him stalking the halls of Edinburgh Castle, watched how people scurried out of his path. Now, trapped in this dank vault, I understood why.

"I don't understand. I work for the Council. Why—"

"Spare me," Cian snapped, his voice like ice, sharp and brittle. He circled my chair. His footsteps echoed off the damp stone, each one stoking the fire of my fear. "We know about your... associations. Your sudden increase in power. Tell me, how long have you been in league with The Morrigan?"

I bit my tongue, swallowing the torrent of questions threatening to spill out. I would never give him answers, no matter how little I knew.

His laugh cut through the air, sharp as a blade. "What's the matter, Edin? Cat got your tongue? And here I thought Council secretaries were supposed to be chatty."

I yanked against my restraints, metal biting into my wrists. "Why did you have your goon kidnap me?"

My eyes darted to the man lurking in the corner. Built like a brick wall, with cold grey eyes and a scar running down his left cheek, he exuded an aura of contained violence. Cian's lips curled into a patronising smile. "Oh, come now. You didn't think we'd let someone of your... newfound abilities wander about unchecked, did you? We're simply taking necessary precautions."

He leaned in close, his breath hot on my cheek. I recoiled, the stench of stale coffee and something metallic — blood? — turning my stomach. His fingers gripped my chin, forcing me to meet his icy gaze.

"So I'll ask one more time." Cian's lips curled into a sneer. "How long have you been in league with The Morrigan?"

"I don't know what you're talking about."

"A fire witch, whose power has suddenly surged beyond anything we've ever seen? Your entrance tests showed nothing close to the charge you're putting out now. Do not insult my intelligence."

Fear clawed at my throat. They knew about the guys. About our bond. Goddess, what had I gotten myself into?

"I want to know everything," Cian continued, his voice low and menacing. "How you made contact with The Morrigan. What she's planning."

My heart thundered in my chest. I thought of Rhydian, of Knox and Finlay. Of the warmth and safety I'd found with them. No matter what happened, I couldn't betray that.

"I don't know anything," I insisted. "Please, just let me go. I haven't done anything wrong!"

Cian sighed with exaggerated disappointment. "I had hoped you would be reasonable, Miss MacKenzie. But if you insist on being difficult..."

He turned to the shadows, nodding to someone I couldn't see. "Declan, she's all yours. Do try to leave her in one piece. We may need her later."

With that, Cian vanished. My breath caught in my throat as my kidnapper stepped into the light, a wicked smile playing across his lips.

"Well, well," Declan purred, circling my chair like a predator stalking its prey. "Aren't you a pretty little thing? Such fire in those eyes. I do so enjoy breaking the spirited ones."

I jerked against my restraints, panic rising. "Stay away from me!"

Declan laughed, the sound echoing off the damp stone walls. "Oh, don't be like that, love. We're going to have so much fun together."

His gloved hand trailed along a nearby table,

lovingly caressing an array of cruel-looking instruments. My stomach turned at the sight.

"Do you know where we are?" he asked conversationally, selecting a wicked-looking blade from the collection. "This vault has quite the history. Centuries of secrets and screams soaked into these very walls." He leaned in close, his breath hot against my ear. "They say you can still hear the echoes, if you listen closely. Shall we add your voice to the chorus?"

I squeezed my eyes shut, desperately wishing for Rhydian to find me like he had with the fire. But the shadows remained stubbornly still, offering no escape.

"I'll ask you one more time," Declan said, pressing the cold edge of the blade against my cheek. "Tell us what we want to know. How did your power grow? What are your ties to The Morrigan?"

"I don't know!" I cried, tears stinging my eyes. "Please, I swear, I don't know anything!"

He tsked, shaking his head in mock disappointment. "Pretty words. Let's see how long they last when the screaming starts. I do love a challenge."

"Please," I begged, my voice breaking. "I'm just a secretary. I don't know anything about The Morrigan or—"

His hand shot out, gripping my chin painfully. "Lies," he hissed. "I can see it in your eyes. You're protecting someone. Those men you've been seen with, perhaps?"

My heart stuttered. How much did they know?

"They're just friends," I lied, praying he couldn't hear the tremor in my voice.

He smiled, cold and cruel. "We'll see about that. They always break, you know. In the end, they beg me to let them spill their secrets."

The blade trailed down my neck, a whisper of steel against skin. "But the strong ones... their screams make the best songs."

Terror clawed at my insides, threatening to consume me. This was it. I was going to die here, alone in this dank vault. I'd never see my soulmates again, never get the chance to tell them...

To tell them what?

In that moment, staring death in the face, everything crystallised with startling clarity. The constant ache in my chest, the pull I felt towards Rhydian, Knox, and Finlay — it wasn't just the bond. It was love. Real, soul-deep, earth-shattering love.

I loved them. All of them. Rhydian's brooding intensity, Knox's easy charm, Finlay's quiet strength. They were a part of me now, as essential as the air in my lungs or the fire in my veins.

And I'd be damned if I let this bastard use that love against them.

I met his gaze, steel in my voice. "Do your worst. I won't tell you anything."

His eyes widened fractionally, surprise flickering across his face before it was replaced by cruel amusement. "Oh, kitten. I was hoping you'd say that."

He turned back to the table of instruments, humming softly to himself as he selected his tools. The sound grated against my nerves, a discordant melody of impending pain.

I closed my eyes, drawing strength from the bond thrumming beneath my skin. My boys were out there somewhere. They'd find me. They had to.

Rhydian, Knox, Finlay. If you can hear me, please... I need you.

Declan footsteps drew closer, and I braced myself for what was to come. No matter what happened, I wouldn't break. I'd protect them with my last breath if I had to.

Because that's what you did for the people you loved.

CHAPTER SIXTEEN

RHYDIAN

"She's gone!" Finlay's panicked voice blared from my phone. "There was a surge of power and now I can't find her anywhere!"

Ice flooded my veins as his meaning sank in. She. Edin. My body tensed, muscles coiling as if the walls were about to come alive with my worst enemies. Only they wouldn't because those same monsters were focused on doing *Annwn* knew what to Edin.

"What do you mean, gone? Where were you?"

I leapt to my feet and paced my bedroom in long, agitated strides, shadows writhing at my feet as my control slipped. My grip tightened on the phone while my mind raced through possibilities, cataloguing my hit list, old scores left unsettled. A surge of power could only mean one thing – someone had taken her.

Someone powerful enough to snatch a witch right out from under Finlay's nose.

"The department store on Princes Street. We were shopping for clothes and—"

I didn't wait to hear the rest. Shadows surged around me, responding to the spike of fear in my chest. In an instant, I was plunging through the void between worlds, emerging in a deserted alley beside the shop.

The bustling street assaulted my senses — the chatter of shoppers, the scent of exhaust and fried food from nearby vendors. I pushed it all aside, focusing on the tenuous thread of the soulbond. It hummed faintly, a lifeline I desperately clung to.

"Thank the Goddess." Finlay stood just inside the store's entrance, wild-eyed and dishevelled. "I don't know what happened. One minute she was here, the next—"

"Show me," I growled, cutting off his rambling.

He led me through the store, weaving between racks of clothes and bewildered shoppers. I scanned every shadow, every corner, searching for a flash of Edin's fiery hair or the warmth of her amber eyes.

"She was trying on clothes," Finlay said as we reached the changing rooms. "I was waiting out here, and then I felt this... surge. Like someone had pulled on the bond. When I called out to her, there was no answer."

I pushed past him into the changing area, ignoring the startled gasp of a woman emerging from one of the cubicles. Edin's scent lingered here — jasmine and smoke, with an undercurrent of something uniquely her. My chest ached at the familiar smell.

"Which one?" I demanded.

Finlay pointed to a cubicle at the far end. I yanked the curtain aside and stepped into the empty space. Clothes lay scattered on the floor, as if dropped in a hurry. And there, clinging to the air like a noxious cloud, was the faintest trace of power.

Familiar power.

"Fuck," I snarled, slamming my fist against the thin partition wall. The entire thing shook while shadows writhed around me, responding to the surge of rage and fear.

"What is it?" Finlay asked, his voice tight with worry. "Do you recognise something?"

I nodded grimly. "Council magic."

And not just any Council magic — this reeks of Cian.

The thought of that sadistic bastard anywhere near Edin made my blood run cold.

Finlay's expression momentarily relaxed, relief washing over his features. But just as quickly, his brow creased and confusion clouded his eyes.

"But why?" Finlay asked. "But why take her at all? What could they possibly want with Edin?"

"Information. About us. About the soulbond."

Finlay's eyes widened. "You don't think they'd..."

"Torture her?" I spat the word like poison. "In a heartbeat."

I kept my suspicions about Cian to myself. No need

to burden Finlay with the ugly details of my past dealings with the Council's most ruthless investigator. The less he knew about that world, the safer he'd be.

Had I convinced myself that her position in the council would spare her? What had I been thinking? Edin's magic was unstable without us. Even if she hadn't chosen to leave, it would have remained dangerous without me if Finlay's research could be believed. She couldn't control her power alone, yet I'd pushed her away, believing distance would keep her safe.

But safe from what? From me? From the dangers that followed us? I'd been so caught up in my own fears that I'd overlooked the most obvious threat — the very council Edin worked for.

My fists clenched at my sides. I'd been a fool, thinking her position would protect her when it made her even more of a target. And now, because of my stubborn pride and misguided attempts at protection, Edin was in danger.

I had to make this right. I had to find her, to save her from the mess I'd helped create.

And this time, I wouldn't push her away. I couldn't afford to make that mistake again.

I closed my eyes, reaching for the soulbond. It pulsed weakly, a fragile thread stretching out into the unknown. Edin was alive, at least. But for how long?

"We need to find her," Finlay said, his voice steadier now. Always the pragmatist. "Can you track her like you did with the fire?"

I pressed my hand to my chest, where the soulbond mark burned beneath my shirt. Memories flashed through my mind — Edin's smile, the way her eyes lit up when she laughed. The bond flared to life, stronger now.

"I can feel her," I breathed. "It's faint, but... she's scared."

The thought of her suffering sent a fresh wave of fury through me. How could I have been so blind? So stubborn? I'd pushed her away, thinking I was protecting her, when all I'd done was leave her vulnerable.

Here's the revised sentence showing Finlay begging Rhydian to find Edin:

"Find her, Rhydian." His voice cracked with a desperation I'd never heard from him before. "Please. Bring her home."

Home.

That one word stirred something inside of me, an emotion I'd tried to bury at some point in my long and shady career.

When had Edin become home? When did they all become so essential to me?

I nodded grimly, already reaching for the shadows. "I'll find her."

The shadows curled around my fingers, eager and hungry.

Finlay stared at me, worry etched into every line of his face. "Be careful. Edin will kill us both if you get yourself hurt trying to play the hero."

A ghost of a laugh escaped me. He was right — our fierce little firecracker would tear us all a new one for putting ourselves in danger. The thought only made my chest ache more fiercely.

I closed my eyes, focusing on the soulbond once

more. It tugged gently, urging me... south? Towards the old town? The shadows envelop me and let the bond guide me like a compass needle, growing stronger with each passing moment.

CHAPTER SEVENTEEN

EDIN

"*H*aving regrets, witch?" Declan sneered, his fake sympathy obvious. He stood by a table full of nasty-looking tools, running his fingers over them. "Wishing you'd taken our offer of leniency?"

His footsteps echoed through the damp vault, each step making my pulse quicken. I tugged at my restraints, the cold metal biting into my wrists. Useless.

I tried to summon my fire, but nothing happened. They must have spelled the cuffs to block my power somehow.

There had to be a way for me to reach the guys. If Rhydian could feel when I was in trouble and find me, I had to be able to use that to our advantage. We'd spent so little time truly exploring our bond, too distracted by each other and my unstable magic. Now, facing torture and possible death, I cursed my own stubbornness.

I swallowed hard, fighting to keep my voice steady. "I told you, I don't know anything about The Morrigan or her plans."

He chuckled, the sound scraping against my nerves. "Oh, I think you do. And even if you don't..." His hand settled on a small, vicious-looking device. "Well, I'm sure we can find other topics to discuss."

My breath caught as he lifted the instrument. It was deceptively simple — two flat pieces of metal connected by a screw. But even in the dim light, I could see the wicked points on its inner surface.

"Do you know what this is?" He held it up, letting it catch the torchlight. "This little beauty is called a thumbscrew. Used quite extensively during the Edinburgh witch trials." His smile was all teeth, no warmth. "Fitting, don't you think?"

A chill ran down my spine. "This particular model," he continued, approaching with measured steps, "is said to have extracted confessions from over a hundred witches. Some true, some false. In the end, it hardly mattered. Pain has a way of making truth... flexible."

"Please," I whispered, hating the tremor in my voice. "You don't have to do this."

I pulled against my chains with growing desperation. My heart pounded so hard I could feel it in my throat.

He tsked, shaking his head. "But I do, witch. It's nothing personal, you understand. Just following orders." He knelt beside my chair, reaching for my hand. "Now, shall we begin?"

Panic surged through me, hot and blinding. My

magic roared to life, desperate to protect me. But my fire sputtered and died before it could manifest.

"Last chance," he said softly, positioning the thumb-screw. "Tell me what you know about The Morrigan, and we can avoid all this unpleasantness."

I met his gaze, steeling myself. "I. Don't. Know. Anything."

He sighed, a sound of exaggerated disappointment. "Very well. Remember, you chose this."

The metal was ice-cold against my skin as he positioned my thumb between the plates. I squeezed my eyes shut, bracing for the pain to come.

Rhydian, Knox, Finlay. I'm sorry. I'm so sorry.

His hand tightened on the screw. I could feel the pressure building, the points digging into my flesh. Any second now, it would—

A furious roar split the air. My eyes flew open just in time to see a mass of writhing shadows explode from the far wall.

Declan whirled, but he was too slow. A dark figure slammed into him, sending them both crashing to the ground in a tangle of limbs and snarling rage.

"Rhydian!" His name tore from my throat, equal parts relief and terror.

I watched in awe as they grappled on the floor. Shadows writhed around them, making it hard to see who had the upper hand. My throat constricted, making it hard to swallow while my pulse thundered in my ears.

Declan planted his feet against Rhydian's chest, kicking him off with surprising force. Rhydian stumbled back, giving the man just enough time to scramble towards the table of weapons.

"Be careful!" I screamed, yanking at my chains. The metal dug into my skin, but I didn't care.

He spun, a wicked-looking dagger clutched in his hand. He slashed wildly and Rhydian dodged, but not fast enough. The blade caught him across the arm, drawing a line of crimson.

I cried out, my heart in my throat.

But Rhydian barely seemed to notice the wound. He lunged forward, grappling for the knife. They struggled, neither willing to give an inch.

"You're too late," Declan spat, his face twisted with malice. "The Council knows about her now. They'll never stop hunting her."

Rhydian growled, a sound more animal than human. "I'll tear apart anyone who tries to touch her."

The man laughed, a harsh, mocking sound. "You can't protect her forever. The Council always gets what it wants in the end."

With a roar of fury, Rhydian twisted the assassin's wrist. The dagger clattered to the floor. In the next instant, Rhydian's fist connected with the man's jaw with a sickening crack.

The fight turned brutal, fists flying, connecting with sickening thuds. Declan fought back, landing a few blows of his own. I flinched each time Rhydian took a hit.

I pulled against my restraints with all my strength, frantic to get to him and do... something. A snap rent the air, the sound alarmingly loud in the confined space.

A spike of hot agony shot up my arm, forcing tears to my eyes. But the adrenaline surging through me compromised my senses, keeping me momentarily numb and disoriented.

The shadows grew thicker, almost alive. They coiled around Declan, constricting like snakes. He gasped and struggled, but Rhydian's power was too strong. I stared in horror as his fist connected with the assassin's jaw, sending him sprawling. The sickening crunch of bone echoed through the room. Before I could process what was happening, Rhydian's hands were around the man's neck.

"Stop!" I cried out, my voice cracking. "You're killing him!"

His eyes met mine, cold and unyielding. In that moment, I saw Rhydian for who he truly was — a dangerous man capable of terrible violence. This wasn't just about protecting me; there was a darkness in him, a ruthlessness that both terrified and thrilled me. If I wanted him, I'd have to accept this part of him too.

"I'd prefer to truss him up and introduce him to his own toys, but we're short on time," he growled. "He doesn't get to walk away from this."

My stomach churned, but I just watched, paralysed, as the life drained from Declan's eyes. His legs twitched, then went still.

Rhydian released his grip, wiping his hands on his jeans like he'd touched something filthy. He stood there for a moment, chest heaving. Then his gaze locked onto mine, and the feral light in them softened.

"Edin," he breathed, crossing the distance between

us in two long strides. His hands cupped my face, so gentle compared to the violence I'd just witnessed. "Are you alright? Did he hurt you?"

I shook my head, not trusting my voice. Tears pricked at my eyes, the events of the past hour — had it truly only been an hour? — catching up to me all at once.

His gaze hardened as he took in the chains binding me, the instruments of torture on the nearby table. A muscle ticked in his jaw.

"I'm getting you out of here."

The shadows responded to his will, coiling around the manacles. For a heartbeat, nothing happened — whatever spell had dampened my magic clearly affected Rhydian's as well. But then the metal groaned, straining against the relentless pressure of shadow. With a bone-jarring crack, the chains shattered. A white-hot lance of agony shot through my broken wrist. I couldn't hold back the strangled cry that tore from my throat. Tears pricked at the corners of my eyes as waves of nause-ating pain radiated up my arm. I cradled the injured limb.

His eyes widened. "What's wrong?"

I tried to speak, but the words caught in my throat. All I could manage was a whimper as I cradled my throbbing wrist.

"Let me see," he said, his voice uncharacteristically gentle. He reached for my arm, but I flinched away.

"Sorry," I gasped. "It's just... it hurts."

A muscle ticking in his jaw. "Your wrist is broken." It wasn't a question. His gaze flicked to the body on the floor, then back to me. "I wish I could bring that bastard back just to kill him again. Slower this time."

The cold fury in his voice sent a shiver down my spine. But beneath it, I could hear something else. Fear. Concern. For me.

"It's okay," I said, trying to sound braver than I felt. "You came. You saved me."

His expression softened, just a fraction. "Always, Star. I'll always come for you."

The intensity in his eyes took my breath away. His proximity sent sparks dancing across my skin, igniting a fire I hadn't felt since that first night.

The intensity in his eyes took my breath away. His proximity sent sparks dancing across my skin, igniting a fire I hadn't felt since that first night.

Before I could think better of it, I surged forward, pressing my lips to his. The moment we connected, my power purred and curled up like a contented cat inside me. Warmth flooded through my body, soothing and overwhelming in how right it felt.

Except... he went utterly still.

He didn't kiss me back. Of course, he didn't. I pulled back, mortified. What was I thinking?

"I'm sorry," I stammered. "I didn't mean to — I just — you were — and I thought—"

But Rhydian wasn't looking at me. His gaze was fixed on some point in the distance, his expression unreadable.

"We need to go," he said, his voice low and tight. "Knox and Finlay are waiting. Cian could return at any moment."

The mention of Cian sent a chill down my spine. I'd almost forgotten about the Council investigator.

"Rhydian, I—"

Before I could finish, shadows swirled around us. The world tilted and spun, and then we were gone, leaving the dank vault, Declan's body, and my confused emotions behind.

CHAPTER EIGHTEEN

RHYDIAN

"*F*ucking hell!"

Knox and Finlay shot to their feet when I stepped out of the shadows into our flat with a shaking Edin clutched to my chest yet again. My muscles ached, every breath sending a sharp pain through my ribs. Probably broken. But none of that mattered. Edin was safe. She was here, in my arms, trembling but alive.

Horror claimed Knox's expression while Finlay shoulders with relief. I didn't need a mirror to know I looked a right state. The ruined shirt, the blood... I'd seen corpses that looked healthier.

"I'm fine," I grunted. "But Edin's wrist is broken."

That snapped them into action. Knox's eyes widened, while Finlay let out a string of colourful curses that would always be out of place falling from the book nerd's lips.

"Edin, love," Knox said softly, approaching us slowly. "Can you hear me?"

She nodded weakly against my chest. I could feel her heart racing, her breath coming in short, sharp gasps. The urge to whisk her away, to hide her somewhere no one could ever hurt her again, was almost over-whelming.

"Put her on the sofa." Finlay knocked a pile of books off the cushion without pause.

I nodded, carefully manoeuvring Edin to the sofa. As I set her down, she whimpered, the sound tearing at something deep in my chest. Her eyes, usually so full of fire, were dull with pain and fear.

"Knox, get the first aid kit," Finlay ordered, his voice tight with worry.

Knox nodded, already moving. "We need more than that," he muttered as he disappeared into the bathroom. "A lot bloody more."

I backed away, giving Finlay space to fuss over Edin. My hands clenched at my sides, useless and trembling. The adrenaline was wearing off, leaving me feeling hollow and raw.

Finlay knelt beside Edin, his hands hovering uncer-tainly. "I'm so sorry," he choked out. "I was right there. I should have done something."

Edin shook her head weakly. "Not your fault," she managed, her voice barely above a whisper. "You couldn't have known."

Knox returned, first aid kit in hand. He shoved it at

me before turning his attention to Edin. "Here, love," he said softly, offering her some painkillers and a glass of water. "This should help take the edge off."

I retreated to a corner, mechanically going through the motions of patching myself up. The familiar routine helped ground me, even as my mind raced.

"We're so sorry, Edin," Knox said, his voice thick with emotion. "We should have suspected something like this might happen. We should have protected you."

She snorted. "Last I checked, you weren't psychic, Knox. Don't beat yourself up," Edin said, a hint of her usual fire returning to her voice. "You're here now. That's what matters." Her gaze found mine across the room. "Thank you, Rhydian. For coming for me."

I froze, caught off guard by the intensity in her eyes. Before I could respond, a low growl cut through the room.

Grimm padded in, his golden eyes fixed on Edin. He leapt onto the sofa, sniffing her carefully. "You're safe now," he rumbled, his tail lashing. "And those Council bastards will pay. I'll tear out their entrails and use them for—"

"Grimm," Edin said, her voice weak and tired. "Please."

The cat huffed but settled in her lap, purring loudly. I watched as Knox and Finlay fussed over her, their hands gentle as they checked her for other injuries. While mine shook as I fumbled with the first aid kit and then poured disinfectant over the cuts on my knuckles, the sting barely registering. All I could think about was that kiss.

Edin's lips on mine, soft and desperate.

In the heat of the moment, with adrenaline pumping through my veins and relief making me weak, I'd frozen. For a second, everything had felt right. Like the final piece of a puzzle clicking into place.

And then reality had come crashing back.

What was I thinking? I was poison. Everything I touched turned to ash. I'd drag her down into the darkness with me, and she deserved so much better than that.

But then... if I hadn't been there, if I hadn't come for her...

"Rhydian?" Edin's voice, small and uncertain, snapped me back to the present. "Are you okay?"

I nodded stiffly, not trusting my voice. Knox shot me a look that said he didn't believe me for a second.

"What happened after they took you?" Finlay asked gently.

She took a shaky breath. "I was in the changing room, and then... someone grabbed me, covered my mouth, and everything went dark." Her voice trembled. "When I woke up, I was in the vaults and they were..." She swallowed hard. "Threatening to torture me."

"The bastards," Knox growled, the sound more animal than man. "I'll kill them all."

I clenched my fists, fighting the urge to hunt down every last Council member right then and there.

"They kept asking about The Morrigan. About our bond. They thought I knew something, that I was working with her somehow. The things they were going to do to me..." A sob caught in her throat.

"Hey, hey." Knox pulled her into his lap, dislodging a disgruntled Grimm. He hugged her tight. "You're safe now. We've got you."

But even as he comforted her, I could see the fury in his eyes, the barely leashed violence. Finlay looked no better, his usually gentle face hard as stone.

"Let me see your wrist," I said gruffly, finally finding my voice. I needed to do something, to channel this rage into action.

Edin hesitated, her gaze dropping to my own battered hands. "You're hurt too. Let me help—"

"No," I said, the word exploding from me harsher than I intended. I softened my voice, trying again. "I'm fine. This is nothing new for me. We need to deal with your wrist first."

"We can't take her to a hospital," Knox said, voicing what we were all thinking. "The Council might be watching."

"I have a friend," Edin said. "She's a doctor. She could help."

"No," I said without thinking. "We can't trust anyone right now."

Edin frowned. "Veronica's my best friend. She'd never hurt me."

"You didn't think the Council would hurt you either." I hated the way she flinched at my words.

"Veronica doesn't work for the Council," she said. "Please, Rhydian. I trust her."

I studied Knox and Finlay, seeing my own conflicted emotions mirrored in their faces. We couldn't afford to trust the wrong person, not now. But the pain etched into every line of Edin's face, the way she cradled her injured wrist against her chest—my resolve crumbled.

"Fine," I growled. "But I'm vetting her first."

Edin nodded, relief clear in her eyes. "Thank you."

As Knox helped Edin make the call, I retreated back to my corner. My mind raced as I methodically cleaned and bandaged the worst of my wounds. The Council knew about us. Knew about the bond. And they were willing to torture Edin for information on The Morrigan. The goddess I had been treating as a nebulous future threat had suddenly become very, very real.

The bond mark on my chest pulsed, warm and insistent. For the first time since it had appeared, I didn't try to ignore it.

I glanced at Edin, at the bruises blooming on her pale skin, the careful way she held herself. This fierce, beautiful woman who had turned my world upside down. At Knox and Finlay, my brothers in all but blood, their faces taut with worry and anger. My resistance to the bond, my belief that staying detached would keep them safe... it all seemed so foolish now.

I had been willing to die for them from the start. Was it really such a leap to live for them too?

The realisation settled over me, heavy and certain. I couldn't keep holding myself apart, not if I wanted to protect them.

My gaze caught hers across the room, and I saw my own resolve reflected back at me. No more running. No more denial.

Once she hung up the call and announced that her

friend would be here in ten minutes, I crossed the room in a few long strides, kneeling in front of her.

"I'm sorry," I said, my voice rough with emotion. "I'm so sorry, Edin. This is my fault."

She frowned. "How could this possibly be your fault?"

I swallowed hard, forcing myself to meet her eyes. "I've been keeping you at arm's length, thinking it would keep you safe. But if I hadn't... if I'd been there with you..."

Edin's uninjured hand found mine, her touch soft and warm. Despite the gentleness, I could sense a new wariness in her, a result of seeing my darker side in action. But she didn't pull away.

"Rhydian, stop. It's not your fault."

"But if I'd been there—"

She cut me off with a snort. "What, you'd have stood in the tiny fitting room with me while I tried on clothes?" Her eyes sparkled with amusement. "I'm not sure the shop assistants would have approved."

Despite everything, a smile tugged at my lips. "I'd have found a way. Shadows are good for more than just travel, you know."

She laughed, then winced as the movement jostled her injured wrist.

"I was wrong," I said, unable to let it slide. The words felt like they were being torn from my chest. "If I'd just accepted it from the start, maybe we would have been prepared. Maybe you wouldn't have gotten hurt."

Knox snorted. "You're giving yourself too much

credit, mate. The Council would have come for us eventually."

"He's right," Finlay added. "This is bigger than just us."

Edin squeezed my hand. "You came for me. When it mattered most, you were there."

I shook my head. "I should have been there sooner. I should have—"

"Stop," Edin cut me off. "You can't change the past, Rhydian. What matters is what we do now. I forgive you, Rhydian. But please, no more pushing me away."

I nodded, squeezing her hand gently. "No more pushing away. I promise. I'll always protect you. All of you. Whatever it takes."

The soulbond mark on my chest pulsed, warm and alive. For the first time, I embraced it fully, letting the connection wash over me.

Edin's eyes widened, a small gasp escaping her as she pressed a hand to her heart. "I can feel you," she whispered. "All of you. It's... it's incredible."

Knox and Finlay nodded, their own expressions filled with wonder. I could feel them too, their presence warm and solid in my mind. It both thrilled and terrified me. I'd spent so long keeping my distance, convinced that my shadows would only bring her harm. But now, seeing her here, safe and whole after nearly losing her, I couldn't deny the pull anymore.

"Can you tell me exactly what they said about The Morrigan?" I asked, my tone growing serious. "Every detail you can remember."

Edin's brow furrowed in concentration. "They kept

asking if I was working for her. They seemed to think our bond was some kind of... I don't know, proof of allegiance?"

My blood ran cold. "They think we're working with her?"

Edin nodded. "They wanted to know her plans, what she was plotting against the Council."

"Did they say anything specific about what they thought those plans might be?" I asked.

"Not really," Edin said. "But they seemed... scared. Like they genuinely believed The Morrigan was about to make some big move against them."

"Bloody hell," Finlay muttered. "If the Council's this spooked, things are worse than we thought."

I sat back on my heels, processing this information. The Council, an organisation I'd always seen as all-powerful and untouchable, was afraid. Of us. Of what our bond might mean.

"There's more to this than we realised," I muttered, more to myself than to Edin. "If Cian's involved, this goes all the way to the top of the Council."

She nodded, her amber eyes serious. "What are we going to do?"

"I don't know yet." I met her gaze, feeling the bond pulse between us. I ran a hand through my hair, mind racing. "But this changes everything. The Council, The Morrigan... we're caught in the middle of something huge."

"And they're willing to torture for information," Knox added, his voice hard.

Edin shuddered, and I found myself reaching for her

hand without thinking. She gripped my fingers tightly, like I was a lifeline.

"It's worse than that," Grimm's voice cut through the tension. We all turned to look at the cat, who was pacing back and forth on the coffee table, his tail twitching agitatedly.

"What do you mean?" I asked, my voice low.

He sighed, a surprisingly human sound coming from the feline. "The Council thinks The Morrigan is preparing for war. They're afraid she's trying to resurrect the Twelve."

Finlay leaned forward, his eyes alight with curiosity. "Who are they?"

"The Morrigan's chosen warriors," Grimm said. "They were meant to close the door between this realm and the god realm. But they were betrayed."

"By who?" Knox asked.

"The thirteenth," Grimm said, his voice heavy with old pain. "A witch who went mad. She was caught by witch hunters, and her family turned against the Twelve. They destroyed them on the night of the ritual, before they could find out what had happened to her or finish sealing the doorway."

Edin's hand tightened in mine. "How do you know all this?" she asked.

Grimm's golden eyes met mine, and I saw centuries of regret in their depths. "Because I was there."

Silence fell over the room as we all processed this information. The implications were staggering. If the Council truly believed The Morrigan was trying to finish what she started centuries ago...

We have to leave," I said abruptly, standing up. "Edinburgh isn't safe for us anymore."

"Leave?" Edin's voice was small. "But... where would we go?"

I ran a hand through my hair, mind racing. "I don't know yet. But we can't stay here. The Council knows where to find us."

"Can we at least wait until morning?" Edin asked, her eyes pleading. "Just one more night here. Please?"

I wanted to argue, to insist we leave immediately. But the exhaustion in her eyes, the way she was still trembling slightly... I couldn't bring myself to push her.

"Fine. But we leave before sunset tomorrow. No exceptions."

Edin nodded, relief washing over her face. "Thank you."

I turned to start packing, but Knox's hand on my arm stopped me. "Hold on a second. Before you go running off, we need to get something straight."

"What?" I asked, impatience seeping into my tone.

Finlay stepped up beside Knox, his expression equally serious. "Does this mean you're all in? No more brooding, no more stalking off in a mood? You're embracing our soulbond and Edin?"

I froze, Knox's question hanging in the air like a knife waiting to drop. Hadn't I made that clear already? Every damn word I'd spat out since we got back screamed that I was ready — no, desperate — to embrace this gift they definitely didn't deserve. No matter how much it messed with my head. But of course, Knox wouldn't let it slide. He never did.

"Yes," I said, my voice firm. "I'm all in. No more running, no more pushing you away. I promise."

"You're sure?" Edin asked, her voice barely above a whisper.

I knelt in front of her again, taking her face in my hands. "I'm sure," I said, pouring every ounce of sincerity I had into my words. "I was an idiot before, and it nearly cost us everything. I won't make that mistake again. You're stuck with me now, Star. All of you."

Edin's smile was blinding, even through her tears. Knox and Finlay wore matching grins, the tension draining from their shoulders.

She leaned forward, pressing her forehead against mine. "Good, because I'm not strong enough to leave you again."

With a lump forming in my throat, I wrapped my arms around her and held her tight.

CHAPTER NINETEEN

EDIN

"*W*hat did you do to yourself, and why did I just get the third degree from the bulky broody guy?" Veronica asked as she burst through the door closely followed by Rhydian.

He'd insisted on meeting her downstairs and "vetting her". Whatever that meant.

Veronica's gaze flicked between my cradled wrist and the two men hovering behind me.

A nervous chuckle escaped my lips. "It's a long story, V. Thanks for coming so fast."

"A long story involving three gorgeous men and a broken wrist?" Her brow wrinkled as she approached me. "Edin, darling, I leave you alone for five minutes..."

Heat crept up my neck. "It's not what you think."

"Oh really?" Veronica arched an eyebrow, setting her bag down on the coffee table. "Because what I think is that my best friend, who I last saw struggling with her magic and contemplating the merits of a one-night stand, is now shacked up with not one, not two, but *three* ridiculously attractive men."

I winced, both from the twinge in my wrist and the accuracy of her assessment. "Okay, maybe it's exactly what you think."

Knox snorted from his perch on the arm of the sofa. "How else did you think you were going to explain this situation, Sparky?"

I glared at him and he chuckled knowing full well that I hadn't thought that far.

Veronica's eyes narrowed at the nickname, but she didn't comment. Instead, she gestured for me to sit on the sofa. "Alright, let's take a look at that wrist. How did this happen, anyway?"

I exchanged a quick glance with Rhydian, who stood like a sentinel by the window. His jaw clenched, and I could practically feel the tension radiating off him.

"I, uh... I fell," I lied, wincing at how pathetic it sounded.

"You fell," she repeated, her tone flat but her brown eyes flashed with mutiny.

"Yep. Clumsy me, you know how it is."

She sighed, gently taking my injured wrist in her hands. "Edin, I've known you since we were kids. You've never been clumsy a day in your life."

I bit my lip, unsure how to respond. The truth too dangerous, too complicated. How could I explain that I'd been kidnapped by the very organisation I worked for? That I'd broken my own wrist trying to escape a sadistic torturer?

"All you need to know is it wasn't one of the guys, okay?"

Veronica continued to stare at me, unconvinced.

"It's safer if you don't know the details," Finlay said softly from where he leaned against the wall. "For all of us."

Her eyes widened and a flicker of understanding passed over her face. She'd seen enough at the hospital to know when to stop asking questions.

"I see," she said, her tone strained. She turned her attention back to my wrist. "Well, let's get this fixed up, shall we?"

I nodded, relief washing over me. Veronica's hands, cool and steady, gently cradled my injured wrist. Her touch was familiar, grounding. It was different from the electricity that coursed through me when I touched Knox, Finlay, or Rhydian, but comforting in its own way.

"This might tingle a bit," Veronica murmured, her eyes fluttering closed.

A soft golden glow emanated from her fingertips. The light seeped into my skin, wrapping around my bones like a warm embrace. Gentle heat flowed through me. It started as a gentle tickle, barely noticeable at first. Then it grew, flowing up my arm like honey, thick and sweet. The sensation wasn't just physical – it reached deeper, soothing away the lingering fear and tension from my ordeal.

I closed my eyes, letting out a shaky breath as Veronica's magic worked its way through my body. The pain faded quickly and for the first time since I'd been kidnapped, I could take a real deep breath.

When Veronica's hands finally stilled and the glow faded, I opened my eyes to find her watching me with a mix of concern and curiosity.

"Better?" she asked softly.

I flexed my wrist, marvelling at the absence of pain. But it was more than that. I felt... whole. Centred in a way I hadn't been in far too long.

"Much better," I said, my voice thick with emotion. "Thank you, V. You have no idea how much I needed that."

Her lips quirked in a knowing smile. "Oh, I think I have some ideas. Your aura's looking a lot clearer now."

I chuckled, shaking my head. Leave it to Veronica to see right through me, in more ways than one.

"So," she said casually, her tone belying the intensity of her gaze, "are you going to introduce me to your... friends?"

I cleared my throat. "Right, of course. Veronica, this is Knox, Finlay, and Rhydian." I gestured to each of them in turn. "Guys, this is my best friend, Veronica."

"Pleasure," Knox said with a wink.

Finlay offered a polite nod. "Thanks for coming to help."

Rhydian remained silent, his eyes fixed on some point in the distance.

Veronica hummed noncommittally, her focus seemingly on checking my wrist's movement. But I knew her too well to be fooled. She was cataloguing every detail, every interaction.

"So, how exactly did you all meet?" she asked, her tone deceptively light.

I swallowed hard. How could I possibly explain the whirlwind of the past few days? The instant connection, the soulbond, the chaos and danger that had followed?

"It's... complicated," I finally managed.

She snorted. "I'll bet. One minute you're lamenting your love life, the next you're playing house with a trio of hunks. That's quite a turnaround, even for you."

Heat burned into my cheeks. "It's not like that, V. Well, not *just* like that."

She raised an eyebrow. "Oh? Do tell."

How could I make her understand when I barely understood it myself?

"Remember how I was having trouble with my magic?"

Veronica nodded. "Hard to forget. You were lighting things on fire left and right."

"Well, it turns out... these guys are the solution to that problem."

Her eyebrows shot up. "Excuse me?"

I winced. "I know it sounds crazy, but it's true. When I'm with them, my magic... stabilises. It's like they anchor me."

Her eyes narrowed, her gaze flicking between me and the three men in the room. "That's... unusual."

I laughed, a slightly hysterical edge to the sound. "You have no idea."

"Actually," Finlay said softly, "it's not as unusual as

you might think. It's just that the knowledge has been... suppressed."

Veronica's hands stilled on my wrist, her eyes widening. "What are you saying?"

I took a deep breath. "V, what do you know about soulbonds?"

Her brow furrowed. "Soulbonds? You mean like in those cheesy romance novels you pretend not to read?"

"They're not..." I blushed. "Nevermind. The point is, they're real. And apparently, we have one."

Her jaw dropped. "We, as in... all four of you?"

I nodded, unable to meet her gaze.

"Holy shit," she breathed. Then, after a moment of stunned silence, "Are you sure about this? I know I said put yourself out there, but I didn't think you'd go and land yourself soulmates."

I couldn't help but laugh at the absurdity of it all. "Trust me, I didn't plan this. But... I've never been more sure of anything in my life."

The conviction in my voice surprised even me. But despite the danger and the sheer impossibility of it all, I knew this was right. These men, this bond — it was everything I'd been missing.

Veronica studied me for a long moment. Whatever she saw there seemed to satisfy her, because she nodded slowly. "I can't say I understand it, but if this is what you want, I've got your back."

Relief washed over me. "Thanks, V. That means a lot."

She smirked. "Just promise me one thing?"

"Anything."

"When this all settles down, I want details. Lots and lots of details."

I groaned, burying my face in my free hand. "V!"

She laughed, the sound lightening the mood in the room. "What? Can you blame a girl for being curious? I mean, look at them!"

I peeked through my fingers, my gaze landing on each of my soulmates in turn. Knox, with his roguish grin and twinkling eyes. Finlay, a gentle smile playing on his lips. And Rhydian, his intense gaze softening as it met mine.

"Yeah," I said softly. "I see them."

Veronica chuckled and stood up. "You're good as new. Just try not to 'fall' again anytime soon, okay?"

I smiled. "Thanks. I owe you one."

She waved off my gratitude. "Please, what are best friends for?"

Guilty unfurled in my gut. The guys didn't want me warning anyone that we were leaving, but how could I just disappear on her?

I took a deep breath. "There's something else I need to tell you."

Her brows rose. "Oh?"

"I have to go away for a while. And I won't be able to contact you."

Veronica's eyes widened, darting between me and the guys. "Are you in some kind of trouble?"

I bit my lip, unsure how to answer. "It's complicated." I winced, hating that word and how much I'd used it. "I can't explain everything, but... it's for the best. For everyone's safety."

She chewed her lip, considering me with concern. "I'm getting the feeling that you're anything but safe."

"I know," I said softly. "But I need you to trust me. Can you do that?"

She studied me for a long moment, then sighed. "I don't have much choice, do I? Just... promise me you'll be careful."

I nodded, relief washing over me. "I promise."

She glanced at Rhydian again, then leaned in close. "He does brood prettily, doesn't he?"

I laughed, relieved. "You have no idea."

Veronica straightened, smoothing her shirt. "Well. I guess I should get going, let you get back to..." She waggled her eyebrows suggestively. "Whatever it was you were doing."

"Veronica!" I swatted at her, feeling my cheeks heat.

She grinned, unrepentant. "What? I'm just saying, three hot guys, all that intense soulmate energy... A girl can't help but wonder."

I shook my head, smiling despite myself. "Go. Before I rescind my friendship permanently."

Veronica laughed, bright and carefree. "As if you could." She sobered then, her expression turning serious. "But really, Edin, if you need anything, anything at all, you find a way to call me, okay? No matter what."

I nodded. "I will. I promise."

With one last meaningful look, Veronica turned and headed for the door. As she passed Rhydian, she paused, pinning him with a glare. "You hurt her, and I'll make you wish you'd never been born. We clear?"

Rhydian met her gaze, unflinching. "I'd die before I let anything happen to her ever again."

She held his stare for a beat longer, then nodded, apparently satisfied. "Good." And then she was gone, the door clicking shut behind her.

I bit my tongue on the urge to call her back. I didn't say goodbye. I didn't tell her I loved her. We'd always been within easy reach of one another, ever since primary school. This would be the first time I couldn't rely on her to rescue me from my self inflicted loneliness.

Rhydian's hand settled on the nape of my neck, reminding me that I'd never be alone, by choice or otherwise, ever again. He massaged my muscles, relieving the tension in my neck.

"Are you all right?" he asked, his voice low and rough with concern.

I leaned into his touch, letting my eyes drift shut. "I am now."

He was silent for a moment, his fingers tracing soothing patterns on my skin. "I'm sorry," he said at last.

I sighed and turned to face him. "I don't want any more apologies." I reached up and cupped his cheek.

He leaned into my palm, his eyes searching mine. "But—"

"No. Kiss me, Rhydian. Please."

He hesitated for a second. Then his mouth was on mine, hot and demanding. I melted into him, my fingers tangling in his hair as I pulled him closer.

This kiss was different from the ones I'd shared with Finlay and Knox. There was a desperation to it, a raw need that sparked and caught like wildfire between us. I poured everything I felt into that kiss, all the love and longing, the fear and the hope.

Rhydian groaned against my mouth, his hands tightening on my waist. He walked me backward until my legs hit the couch, and then he was lowering me down, his body covering mine.

I gasped as his weight settled over me, delicious and heavy. My hands roamed the broad expanse of his back, feeling the play of muscle beneath his shirt.

"Edin," he breathed, his lips trailing hot kisses down my neck. "My beautiful, brave Edin."

I arched into him, my head falling back to give him better access. "Yours," I agreed, the word a sigh. "Always yours."

He shuddered above me, his hips rocking forward. I could feel the hard length of him pressing against my thigh, and I ached with wanting him.

"Make love to me, Rhydian," I whispered, my hands sliding under his shirt to caress the warm skin beneath. "I need you. All of you."

He drew back to look at me, his eyes dark and heated. "Are you sure?"

I nodded, holding his gaze. "I've never been more sure of anything."

He kissed me again, deep and thorough, and I lost myself in the taste and feel of him. In the overwhelming rightness of his touch, his scent, his presence.

CHAPTER TWENTY

RHYDIAN

For years, I'd held myself apart, convinced that my darkness would taint anyone who got too close. But Edin... she embraced me as I was, without fear. I kissed her, deep and thorough, losing myself in the taste of her. Every nerve in my body sang with the rightness of her touch, her scent, her presence.

My hands roamed her curves, memorising every dip and swell. She arched into my touch, a soft moan escaping her lips. The sound sent a jolt of electricity straight through me, and I growled low in my throat.

"Bedroom," I said, my voice hoarse. "Now."

Without waiting for a response, I scooped Edin into my arms. She let out a surprised squeak, her arms wrapping around my neck. Knox and Finlay followed as I carried her down the hall.

I kicked open the door to my room, grateful that I'd

left it ajar earlier. The space was spartanly decorated, with little more than a large bed and a few necessary pieces of furniture. But right now, the only thing that mattered was the woman in my arms and the two men following close behind.

I stepped into the dimly lit room, cradling Edin against my chest. Her warmth seeped through my shirt, igniting a fire in my veins. Knox and Finlay trailed behind, chuckling.

I shot them a withering glare. "Shut it."

Their grins only widened, clearly enjoying my discomfort. I laid Edin gently on the bed, my breath catching at the sight of her fiery hair spread across my dark sheets. She looked up at me, her lips curved in a soft smile that made my heart ache.

I tugged my ruined t-shirt over my head, tossing it aside. The cool air kissed my skin as I crawled onto the bed, my eyes locked on Edin. Her gaze wandered over my tattooed chest, sending a shiver down my spine.

I captured her lips in another searing kiss, pouring days of pent-up longing into it. She responded with equal fervour, her fingers tangling in my hair. Lost in the moment, I almost forgot we weren't alone.

Breaking the kiss, I glanced over my shoulder. Knox and Finlay still hovered by the door, their expressions a mix of desire and uncertainty.

"If you want in on this," I said, "get your asses over here. Now."

Knox chuckled, already shrugging off his jacket. "Don't have to tell me twice."

Finlay grinned, following suit. "Thought you'd never ask."

They approached the bed, shedding their clothes with urgency. I turned back to Edin, drinking in the sight of her. Her chest rose and fell rapidly, her lips swollen from our kiss.

"You okay with this?" I asked softly, needing to be sure.

She nodded, her eyes bright with desire. "More than okay."

I kissed her again, slower this time. The bed dipped as Knox and Finlay joined us, their hands roaming over Edin's body.

A low moan escaped her lips, muffled against my mouth. The sound sent a jolt of heat straight to my groin. I pulled back, watching as Knox nipped at her neck while Finlay's fingers danced along her thigh.

"Perfect," I murmured, my voice thick with emotion.

And she was. Sprawled across my bed, surrounded by the three of us, Edin looked like a goddess come to life. A goddess who'd chosen us, despite all our flaws and my darkness.

I vowed then and there to never take this gift for granted again.

We made quick work of her clothing, striping her bare to our wandering hands and lips.

This was so far beyond anything I'd ever allowed myself to imagine. The depth of emotion threatened to overwhelm me, but for once, I didn't fight it.

As the last piece of clothing hit the floor, a pulse of energy rippled through the room. Our soulbond marks began to glow, casting a soft purple light that danced across our skin. The sight of it took my breath away.

"It's beautiful," Edin whispered, her fingers tracing the mark on my chest.

I covered her hand with mine, pressing it firmly against my thundering heart. "You're beautiful."

With a thought, I called forth my shadows, letting them curl around her wrists and ankles, pinning her gently to the bed.

"Is this okay?" I murmured, searching her face for any sign of discomfort.

She nodded eagerly. "God, yes."

Her eyes widened as they took on a life of their own, caressing and teasing her skin. They danced over her nipples and tracing delicate patterns along her inner thighs, creating temporary, beautiful markings that heightened her arousal. These marks were sensitive to touch.

Edin gasped as Knox traced one of the designs with his tongue. Then my shadows flicked across her clit and her back arched off the bed. I captured her mouth in another kiss, swallowing her moans.

"It's like her nerves are on the surface," Knox murmured.

I commanded my shadows to explore further, and Edin's eyes widened as they teased her entrance, writhing and pulsing against her delicate flesh. She cried out as they filled her, her body convulsing around the shadowy invasion. I pulled back, watching her writhe in pleasure, my own desire throbbing in time with her movements.

Finlay leaned in and whispered, "Not yet, Firefly. Hold it back just a little longer." Edin groaned in frustration, thrashing under the restraint of my shadows, but her body obeyed.

"Please," she begged.

Knox chuckled low in his throat. "Someone's eager." His eyes met mine, a wicked gleam in them. "Mind if I join in?"

I nodded, curious to see what he had in mind. Knox closed his eyes, concentrating. Sleek, dark tentacles sprouted from his back. They writhed in the air for a moment before reaching for Edin.

She gasped as they made contact with her nipples, her back arching off the bed. "Oh!"

"Too much?" Knox asked, smirking.

Edin shook her head frantically. "No, no. It's perfect. Don't stop."

Finlay whispered in her ear again, planting ideas that heightened her response, making every nerve-ending more sensitive. His eyes met mine, a wicked gleam in them.

Then he claimed her lips in a deep kiss. His hands roamed her body, teasing and caressing. His eyes flashed and Edin's responses intensified. Knox and I shared a smirk. Fin had decided to pull out all of the stops, using his suggestion power on our bodies. Each touch felt more intense, every nerve-ending more sensitive.

I lay down between her legs and settled in to tease my first orgasm from her, using nothing more than the lightest touch of my fingers and the pulse of shadows inside of her.

It didn't take long before she was writhing on the bed again, moaning nonsensical demands.

"Come for me, Star," I commanded, my voice rough with desire. "Let me see you fall apart."

My shadows continued to tease her, drawing out her release until she was left panting and sated on the bed.

I positioned myself between her legs, the sight of her glistening entrance under the low light a vision of perfection. Knox and Finlay moved to her sides, their hands caressing her body as I finally thrust into her. The feel of her tight, wet heat gripping me was almost too much. I groaned, my head falling to her shoulder as I fought the urge to come right then and there.

"Fuck, you feel incredible," I growled against her skin, unable to hold back.

"So do you," she whispered, her breath hot on my neck.

Our movements were frantic, each thrust bringing us closer together. Knox and Finlay took turns kissing her, tweaking her nipples, teasing her sensitive spots, all the while whispering dirty and reverent words of praise in her ear.

"You're doing so good, baby. Taking it all, feeling so fucking perfect," Knox murmured, his fingers trailing down her stomach to where we were joined. Finlay leaned in, whispering ideas into her ear.

Edin's eyes fluttered closed, her head falling back as she surrendered to the combined pleasure. I continued to thrust into her, my shadows coiling around us, enhancing every sensation. As her next orgasm built, I slowed my movements, drawing out the moment, prolonging the torture of sweet anticipation.

Time seemed to slow and stretch, each moment lasting an eternity and yet passing in the blink of an eye. I mapped every inch of Edin's body with my hands and mouth, committing every gasp and shiver to memory.

It wasn't enough.

Knox's eyes flashed with wicked delight. "Someone's hungry for more," he purred, his fingers dancing over her sensitive skin. "Do you want two of us to fill you again? Once my tentacles prepare you?"

Two of us inside her, filling her completely. I stared down at Edin, her face flushed with desire, her eyes clouded with pleasure. "Would you like that?" My fingers teased her clit while my thrusts slowed. "Want Knox to stretch you open for us?"

She nodded eagerly, her breath coming in short gasps. "Yes, please."

I shifted onto my back, pulling Edin onto my lap so she straddled me. Her knees sank into the bed on either side of my hips. I meant to hold her still while he worked, but Edin had other ideas. With a firm grip on my length, she sank down, her eyes falling shut on a shiver.

I barely had it under control before the feel of her velvety walls clenching around me stoked a desperate need to move. I started thrusting into her again, driven by an insatiable hunger for more.

Fucking hell. How had I resisted her for four days?

❋

*E*din
　　Knox caressed my back entrance, teasing
me with slick fingers while Rhydian slammed into me
from below. Every movement seemed to hit the right
spot, sending sparks of delight dancing across my
nerves, the stretching sensation only adding to the intensity. His rhythm was intense, driving deep inside me,
making my breath catch in my throat.

Then he stopped. I protested when he lifted me,
letting his cock slip free. He held me against his chest
and whispered, "Patience, little one."

"Trust us, Edin," Finlay said, his voice low and
soothing, his hand gently rubbing my back.

Knox's tentacles danced around my back entrance,
slick and insistent, before pushing past the rim. My body
tensed at the still new intrusion, the sensation no longer
strange but still foreign. Rhydian held me close, his
breath warm against my neck.

"Breathe, Star," he said. "Just focus on your
breaths."

I did as he said, focusing on their calm presence and
the love flowing through our bond. With a twinge of
discomfort, Knox's tentacle passed through my body's
final barrier. It filled me completely, stimulating spots I
never knew existed. I gasped at the intensity, my vision
momentarily blurring as stars danced behind my closed
eyelids.

"Gods, always so fucking tight," Knox groaned. The
tentacle pulsed and writhed inside me, stroking my sensi-

tive walls as it expanded and contracted. "I'll never get tired of this."

I shivered as the appendage thickened, a soft whimper escaping me. Rhydian's strong arms wrapped around me, holding me steady as Knox thrust the tentacle in and out. He kissed my neck, my collarbone, raining love and comfort upon me.

Rhydian shifted beneath me, repositioning us so his hard cock nudged at my entrance. Grasping my hips, he rolled me forward, coating his length in my arousal. With one swift motion, he thrust back into me, filling my pussy as Knox continued to stretch my ass with his tentacle. The sensation of being filled in both places was overwhelming, a heady mix of pleasure and pain. My body convulsed, muscles clenching around their lengths.

I pushed back from Rhydian's chest, hesitantly rolling my hips to see if I could even move when stuffed so full.

Wasting no time, Finlay reached for me, his clever hands teasing and pinching my nipples, adding to the overload of sensation. His eyes flashed like they had earlier. Only then, I'd been too consumed with need to pay attention. The sensations coursing through my body intensified and I put two and two together.

"You're using your other power on me."

Finlay nodded, a hesitant look in his eyes. "Do you like it?"

"Goddess, yes."

He smiled and his eyes flashed again. My eyelids fluttered as sensation blasted me, every touch intensified.

Knox and Rhydian began to thrust in earnest, Knox's tentacles plunging in as Rhydian's withdrew. I cried out, my body shaking. It was too much, yet not enough. I couldn't help but crave more, needing them to push me to the brink.

"That's it, Firefly." Finlay tweaked my nipples. "Take it all like a good girl."

Panting, I nodded. "More. Need more."

"We'll give you more," Rhydian said, his voice hoarse. "So much more."

With renewed vigour, they continued their relentless dance of lust, each man aiming to push me higher, further into the realm of pleasure and passion. Rhydian's thick cock filled my pussy, creating a delicious friction with each powerful thrust, while Knox's tentacle invaded my ass, expanding and contracting in a symphony of strange and delightful sensations.

Finlay's skilled hands tended to my sensitive nipples, eliciting soft cries and shudders from my overstimulated body. He seemed content to tease me and watch, but I couldn't let him sit on the sidelines.

I reached out and wrapped my hand around his cock and squeezed. He gasped as I stroked him. His erection throbbed in my grasp. He leaned forward, capturing one of my nipples between his teeth while I tightened my grip, delighting in the way his groans of pleasure vibrated against my skin.

"She's ready," Knox said before he withdrew his tentacles.

Rhydian shared a look with him over my shoulder. Finlay pulled out of my grasp and I frowned at them all. They ignored me while Knox and Finlay traded positions and Rhydian shuffled us down the bed until he lay flat on his back. Then he tugged me down to his chest with a soft, amused smile.

"Be a good girl, Edin, and hold still," Rhydian whispered in my ear, his voice deliciously growly. He lifted me once again, letting his cock almost slip free of my pussy.

Finlay squirted more lube on my back entrance and my eyes widened.

Knox's eyes sparkled with mischief as he stroked himself in front of me. "We're not doing anything you can't handle, Sparky."

With a deep breath, I steeled myself and forced my body to relax. Finlay rubbed the lube in and then notched his cock at my back entrance. He thrust forward slowly, feeding me his thick length inch by inch. The added girth was a shock, and I couldn't suppress a gasp as he continued to push deeper.

It felt... strange, stranger than the tentacle, but not entirely unpleasant. Each inch he claimed made my body adjust, my muscles stretching to accommodate the intrusion.

Rhydian's shadows coiled around my breasts, teasing my nipples, amplifying the pleasure coursing through my veins.

Once he was fully seated, I took a moment to catch my breath. Rhydian's shadows danced across my skin, caressing and teasing, heightening every touch and thrust. Every brush of his fingers sent electric shocks of pleasure through me. His fingers tangled in my hair, pulling my head back to stare into my eyes.

Whatever he saw reassured him. He kissed me and then with a firm grip on my hips, he thrust into me again.

As Rhydian and Finlay fucked me, their movements in perfect sync, Knox nudged my lips with his hard cock. I parted my lips and let him in.

He claimed my mouth with short, measured thrusts that almost distracted me from the overwhelming fullness. I whimpered around his cock, the sound muffled by his invasion.

Finlay anchored my hips, driving into me from behind as Rhydian filled my pussy with relentless strokes. Each thrust from one man seemed to echo through the other, creating a symphony of pleasure and pain. Knox's cock hit the back of my throat, as he fucked my face with equal fervour.

As their rhythm intensified, the air in the room thickened with desire and anticipation. My body was a whirlwind of sensations, their touches like sparks igniting the air around us. Rhydian's shadows danced across my skin, caressing and teasing, heightening every touch and thrust.

Rhydian's deep, powerful strokes opposed Finlay's slow, steady thrusts, contrasting with Knox's relentless pounding on my lips. Each man was a master of their craft, wielding their bodies like weapons against my sanity, pushing me closer to the edge with every movement.

"That's it," he growled. "Take us. Milk us. Let us make you feel incredible."

The bed creaked and groaned under the weight of

our frantic movements, the rhythmic slap of flesh against flesh filling the room.

I whimpered around Knox's cock. I writhed and twisted, trying to find some sort of release from the insistent pressure building in my body.

Rhydian gripped my hips tighter, slamming into me with every ounce of his strength. Finlay was unrelenting, driving deeper and harder with each powerful thrust.

My orgasm hit hard, blinding in its intensity. I screamed around Knox's cock, my body convulsing as the overwhelming waves of pleasure washed over me. Rhydian and Finlay roared in sync with my release, their movements erratic.

Rhydian's cock pulsed inside me as he came with a hoarse groan. Finlay pulled out of me, coating my back and thighs with his release. Knox pulled out of my mouth, shooting his load across my face and chest as he bellowed in satisfaction.

I collapsed onto Rhydian's chest, completely spent and wracked with aftershocks. My breathing was ragged, my body limp and sated. Knox slipped off the bed and disappeared into the bathroom while Finlay collapsed beside us and stared up at the ceiling with a dazed look in his eyes.

Rhydian's heart pounded under my ear, each beat echoing through my body. The soulbond thrummed with an overwhelming sense of satisfaction and approval. It was as if the connection had come alive, embracing and nurturing our newfound union.

His shadows gently caressed my skin, soothing and comforting me, mimicking the tender touch of a lover.

They brushed the hair from my face and traced the curve of my cheek, coaxing a soft sigh from my lips.

Knox returned from the bathroom, the sound of dripping water the only break in the heavy silence. He climbed back onto the bed and began to gently clean the mess from my back and thighs.

"Sorry about that," I mumbled, too relaxed to feel even slightly embarrassed by the mess they'd left me in.

"You look good covered in our cum." Finlay said, a smirk in his voice.

"Give us half an hour and we'll do it all over again." Rhydian stroked my hair, pressing a kiss to my forehead.

I couldn't help but laugh at them. If this was what the rest of our lives would be like, I'd die a happy woman.

Once my back was clean, Knox turned me over and nudged me off Rhydian's chest. I protested but only for a second. He dropped a spare cloth on Rhydian and focused on swabbing at my lips and cheeks before chasing his cum down my chest.

Staring up into Knox's amused gaze, I couldn't deny the sense of fulfilment that swelled within me. The bond between us seemed to hum with a newfound energy, as if this intimate act had deepened our connection in ways I couldn't yet understand.

"Edin!" A voice shouted, full of urgency.

I froze, every muscle in my body tensing.

CHAPTER TWENTY-ONE

EDIN

"*B*loody hell! I didn't expect to find you in the middle of... whatever this is!" Hamish's astral form flickered. He averted his eyes, his expression reddening just like mine.

I scrambled to pull the sheets up, desperately trying to cover my naked body. "Hamish! What are you doing?" I shrieked, my voice cracking with panic. "How did you even... what are you doing here?"

Of all the times for my estranged brother to suddenly reappear in my life, it had to be now — naked and sated in the arms of my three soulmates. The universe clearly had a twisted sense of humour.

Knox let out a startled curse, nearly toppling off the edge of the mattress in his haste to sit up. Finlay yelped, grabbing for any scrap of fabric to cover himself. Rhydian, ever the protector, had already conjured shadows to conceal us, his body tense and ready for action.

"I... uh... I didn't realise you'd have company," Hamish stammered.

"You better have a damn good reason for this interruption," Rhydian said, his tone low and menacing.

"The Council. They—" He ran a hand through his hair, a nervous tic he'd had for as long as I could remember. "They came to see me. They were asking questions and—"

My blood ran cold. "What? When?"

"Earlier today," Hamish said, his astral form flickering slightly. "They showed up at my place with a million questions about you." His eyes darted between us again, realisation dawning. "But I see you've been... occupied."

I ignored the jab, focusing on the more pressing issue. "What exactly did they ask?"

Hamish's projection wavered, as if buffeted by an unseen wind. "They wanted to know if I'd seen you recently, if you'd mentioned anything about increased powers or... connections to higher beings."

Rhydian cursed under his breath.

"Did you tell them anything?" Finlay asked, his voice uncharacteristically sharp.

"Of course not," Hamish said, almost sounding insulted. "I'm not about to hand her over to those vultures. Particularly when they start asking questions about The Morrigan." His gaze softened as it landed on me. "This is bad. Whatever you've gotten yourself into... it's big. The Council members who came—they weren't just any lackeys. These were high-ranking officials."

A chill ran down my spine. It hadn't occurred to me that they would go after him, my only remaining family. It should have. They were relentless, ruthless. I knew that better than anyone.

"I'm so sorry. I never meant to drag you into this."

Hamish snorted. "I'll admit I was shocked that the Witches Council would turn up on my doorstep after you." He smiled, the gesture more sad than happy. "It's usually me causing the Council problems. Do I want to know what you did?"

I shook my head, a humourless laugh escaping me. "It's a long story, Hamish. One I'm not even sure I fully understand yet."

"Who exactly are you?" Rhydian asked, his tone guarded, protective. He'd moved to stand between Hamish's astral form and the bed, shadows swirling around him.

"Edin's brother." Hamish eyed Rhydian warily. "And you are?"

"Her soulmate."

Hamish's brows shot up, his gaze sweeping over all four of us again. "Soulmate? As in... oh. Oh, I see." He let out a low whistle. "A new soulbond. That explains why the Council seemed so desperate."

"You know about soulbonds?" Knox asked, surprise evident in his voice.

Hamish nodded. "I'm a historian specialising in ancient magical practices. There's not much about the gods and their gifts I don't know."

Pride for my brother rushed through me, mixed with a twinge of regret for all the years we'd lost. "Hamish, I—"

He held up a hand, cutting me off. "We can catch up later, Red. Right now, we need to focus on keeping you safe. The Council won't stop coming after you, especially now that they suspect your connection to The Morrigan."

Finlay leaned forward. "What do you know about her?"

Hamish's expression turned grave. "More than most. And if what I suspect is true, you four are in more danger than you realise. I'm fairly certain they know about the prophecy."

"Prophecy?" Knox sat up, concern colouring his expression. "What prophecy?"

"If the translations are correct, then one day The Morrigan will come to earth, free Witchkind and remake the thirteen dimensions," he whispered the words with the zeal of a true believer. If I hadn't grown up with him muttering about strange things, it might have scared me. "Only she won't do it alone. There would be an army of allies waiting for her. Allies who had been marked with the serch bythol and their power super juiced from their connection to the Goddess."

I felt the blood drain from my face. "Me. You mean me."

Hamish nodded. "You and others like you. The Morrigan's chosen."

"But I'm just a—" I stopped myself. I wasn't 'just' anything anymore, was I? Not after what I'd been through. Not with this power thrumming through my veins. "How could I possibly be part of this?"

"You're so much more than you realise," Finlay said softly. "You always have been."

"But why? What's the point of all of this?"

"The point," Hamish said, "is love. Connection and a power jump so strong that when grouped with The Morrigan's Twelve, the Gods hidden on earth and the Witches Council wouldn't stand a chance at stopping her from remaking all of existence."

I shook my head, trying to clear it. "This is... it's too much. I can't think about prophecies and armies right now."

"You're right." Rhydian's jaw clenched. "We're leaving. Now. Within the hour."

"What?" I scrambled off the bed, dragging the duvet with me. Shock momentarily overrode my fear. "But we agreed to wait until morning. Can't we at least—"

"No," Rhydian cut me off, his tone brooking no argument. "If they've gone to your brother. I don't trust them not to try and take you again. We can't risk staying any longer."

Knox nodded, his usual easygoing demeanour replaced by grim determination. "Rhydian's right. We need to move fast."

I looked to Finlay, hoping for some support, but he was already up, pulling on his jeans. "I'll start packing the essentials," he said, not meeting my gaze.

My head spun. This was happening too fast. We'd had a plan — wake up early, pack our things, tie up loose ends. Now, in the span of a few minutes, every-thing had changed. Again.

"Fine." I sighed. "But you need to go underground too, Hamish. If they came to you once, they might come back. And after what they did to me..." I shuddered, unable to finish the thought.

He smiled, but it didn't reach his eyes. "Don't worry about me, little sister. I'm already in a safehouse. The Council won't find me."

"Good. That's... that's good." Relief flooded through me, but it was short-lived. "But there's so much I need to tell you, so much that's happened—"

"Another time. I promise," Hamish said, his form starting to flicker more rapidly now. "I'm running out of time. But I need you to know—I'm sorry. For everything. I should have tried harder to keep you away from the Council."

Tears pricked at my eyes. "No, I'm sorry. You were right about them all along, and I was too stubborn to see it. And now they've come for you too."

He smiled, sad and warm. "We were both idiots. But that's family for you, right?"

I laughed, the sound choked with emotion. "Yeah, I guess so."

"Be safe, little sister," Hamish said, his form growing fainter. "And remember—what you have with them, it's real. The bond doesn't create feelings. Trust in that."

With those final words, his astral projection faded away, leaving behind only the faint scent of ozone and the heavy weight of everything left unsaid.

For a moment, I sat frozen, the sheet clutched to my

chest. The room buzzed with frantic energy as the guys moved around me, gathering clothes and essentials.

We were leaving. Now. Tonight. Possibly forever.

"Edin." Rhydian's firm but gentle voice broke through my stupor. He stood in front of me, fully dressed, concern etched in the lines of his face. "We need to move. Can you pack what you need?"

I nodded mutely, finally spurring myself into action. The full weight of the situation settled on my shoulders. This wasn't just about our soulbonds anymore. We'd unwillingly stepped into something much bigger than ourselves.

"What about Veronica?" I asked, my voice small as I pulled on my jeans. "And my job?"

A strange mix of emotions washed over me. Relief, for escaping an organisation I now knew to be corrupt. Fear, for the unknown future that lay ahead. I'd spent years building my career at the Witches Council, believing I was part of something important. Now, in the span of a few days, that illusion had been shattered.

"They know you wouldn't be stupid enough to set foot in Holyrood ever again," Knox paused in his frantic packing to look at me, his eyes softening with sympathy. "We'll figure it out, love. But right now, we need to focus on getting out of here safely."

I nodded, forcing myself to compartmentalise. Safety first. Emotions later.

As I moved around the room, gathering what few possessions I had here, my mind raced. Where would we go? How long would we be gone? Would I ever see Edinburgh again?

My gaze fell on each of my soulmates in turn. Knox, usually so carefree, now moved with a determined purpose I'd never seen before. Finlay, typically lost in his books, was still just as methodical but he carried himself with a newfound confidence. And Rhydian, who had been so closed off just days ago, kept glancing at me with open concern in his eyes.

The flat buzzed with activity. Drawers slammed, zippers whirred, and muffled curses filled the air as we scrambled to pack our lives into a few bags. I caught glimpses of the others as we moved — Knox shoving clothes haphazardly into a duffel, Finlay carefully wrapping what looked like magical artefacts in cloth, Rhydian methodically checking and loading weapons I hadn't even known he owned.

My heart clenched. Just hours ago, we'd been laughing, loving, revelling in our newfound connection. Now, we were preparing to run for our lives.

"Edin." Finlay's voice drew me from my thoughts. He stood in the doorway, a backpack slung over one shoulder. "Do you need help with anything?"

I shook my head, glancing around the room. "I think I've got everything I need here." It wasn't much—some clothes Finlay had had the foresight to buy after the Council snatched me and Grimm. The realisation of how little I now owned hit me.

How had my entire life been reduced to the contents of a single bag and a familiar?

I'd even lost my mother's grimoire in the fire.

The weight of everything we were leaving behind crashed over me. My carefully constructed life, my plans

— all of it was gone. And in its place was this wild, unpredictable future with three men I barely knew but somehow loved more than I thought possible.

"It's a lot to take in, isn't it?" Finlay said softly, as if reading my thoughts.

I nodded. "I just... I don't understand how I could be part of something so important. I'm just... me."

Finlay pulled me into a tight embrace. "You're pretty important to me. To all of us."

I buried my face in his chest, fighting back tears. "But that's different. Being important to you three doesn't mean I'm cut out for... for whatever this prophecy thing is."

"Maybe not," Finlay said softly, his hand rubbing soothing circles on my back. "But it means you're not alone in this. You've seen Rhydian in action, do you think he'd let anything happen to any of us?"

I pulled back, meeting his gaze. "How can you be so calm about all this?"

A wry smile tugged at his lips. "Oh, trust me, I'm terrified. But I've spent my whole life reading about adventures. Now I finally get to live one. With you."

His words warmed something deep inside me. I stood on my tiptoes, pressing a quick kiss to his lips.

"It's going to be okay," he whispered.

A sharp whistle from the living room caught our attention. "Two minutes!" Rhydian called.

"Can you stop with the fucking countdown?" I snapped, my temper flaring. "We're moving as fast as we can!"

As soon as the words left my mouth, I tensed,

waiting for the inevitable burst of uncontrolled fire that had been plaguing me for days. But nothing happened. No flames, no sparks, not even a wisp of smoke.

"What..." I stared at my hands in disbelief.

Finlay grinned. "You accepted the soulbond, remember? It stabilised your power."

I blinked, stunned by this revelation. For the first time in over a week, I felt truly in control of my magic. It was an incredible feeling.

"I'm sorry," I said, the fight draining out of me. "I didn't mean to snap. It's just..."

"Hey," Finlay said softly, cupping my face in his hands. "It's okay. We're all stressed."

From the other room, I heard Rhydian's deep chuckle. "If a bit of swearing is the worst we get from you, we're doing pretty well, Star."

I couldn't help but laugh, the tension breaking. "I'll try to keep the f-bombs to a minimum."

"Don't you dare," Knox called out, his voice light despite the situation. "I love it when you get feisty."

I rolled my eyes, but I was smiling. Even in the midst of this hell, they had a way of grounding me, of making everything feel... right.

Finlay squeezed my hand once before releasing me. "Do you need any help?"

I shook my head and he left to gather up his bags. I took one last look around the room. My gaze lingered on the rumpled bed, still bearing the imprints of our bodies, the lingering scent of our lovemaking. How quickly everything had changed.

With a deep breath, I shouldered my bag, picked

Grimm up and stepped out into the hallway. My familiar looked less than pleased about being woken, but I'd never leave the grumpy bastard behind.

The living room was a flurry of activity. Knox was shoving food into a cooler while Rhydian poured over what looked like a map spread across the coffee table. Finlay emerged from his room, arms laden with books and magical implements.

"Alright," Rhydian said, looking up as I entered. His eyes softened slightly when they met mine, but the urgency in his voice remained. "We've got about thirty seconds. Last chance to grab anything essential."

I glanced around the flat, my chest tightening. This place had become a home in such a short time. The worn leather couch where we'd cuddled and talked. The kitchen where Knox had made us breakfast, still a burnt out shell after I lost control. The bookshelves overflowing with Finlay's collection.

It all felt so familiar, so safe.

And we were leaving it behind.

A lump formed in my throat as the reality of our situation hit me full force. I studied the three of them, my heart heavy. "Are you mad at me?"

They all turned to me, confusion written across their faces.

"Mad at you?" Knox asked. "Why on earth would we be mad at you?"

I swallowed hard, fighting back tears. "Because you have to leave your lives behind. Your jobs, your friends... all because of me."

Finlay was the first to reach me, pulling me into a tight hug. "Oh, Edin. No. Never."

"We're not mad at you," Rhydian said, his voice gruff but gentle. "None of this is your fault."

Knox nodded. "Besides, we're part of this soulbond too, remember? We're just as much of a problem for the Council."

"But your lives..."

"Our lives are with you now," Finlay said, pulling back to look me in the eye. "Everything that matters is right here in this room."

Knox grinned, some of his usual playfulness returning. "Yeah, and let's be honest, my job was boring as hell anyway. This is way more exciting."

Despite everything, I couldn't help but laugh. "Only you would find running for our lives exciting."

Rhydian stepped closer, his hand coming to rest on the small of my back. "We love you, Edin."

My eyes widened, but hope unfurled in my chest. "You do?" They all nodded. "But this is all so new."

Knox chuckled, his blue eyes twinkling. "Love doesn't follow a timeline, Firefly. Sometimes it just hits you like a bolt of lightning."

"Or a soulbond," Finlay added with a wry smile.

I bit my lip, overwhelmed by the surge of emotion. For so long, I'd felt like a piece of me was missing, a hollow ache I couldn't explain. Now, surrounded by these three incredible men, I felt whole for the first time in my life. It was exhilarating and terrifying all at once.

"I love you too," I whispered. "All of you. I realised it when... when I thought I might never see you again."

A hint of a smile on Rhydian's lips. "Now that that's settled, can we please get the hell out of here?"

We all nodded, gathering our bags. Rhydian held me close while Finlay and Knox crowded close to us, gripping each other tightly.

"Ready?" he asked.

We all nodded. Rhydian leaned in, giving me a quick, fierce kiss. Then, with a deep breath, his shadows swirled around us, cool and comforting. As the lights of the flat faded away, I couldn't help but smile. We might be running for our lives, facing dangers I couldn't even imagine, but at least I had the best guys in the world to go into hiding with.

EPILOGUE 1

EDIN

Six months later

"With this cord, I bind your lives as one."

The priestess' words rang through the secluded forest grove as she completed the final knot in the silken cords encircling my wrists — cords that now also encircled the wrists of my three beloved soulmates. Rhydian to my left, Knox to my right, Finlay completing our circle.

A shiver ran through me, and it wasn't just from the crisp autumn breeze that rustled the red-gold leaves above us. No, this shiver came from something deeper — the thrumming, pulsing energy of our soulbond, that mystical tie that had brought the four of us together six months ago in a twist of fate orchestrated by the Morrigan herself.

Six months.

It felt like both an eternity and no time at all. So

much had changed since that night in the Edinburgh pub, when a desperate, unstable fire witch had locked eyes with a brooding assassin, a charming shapeshifter, and a brilliant librarian across a crowded room. I never could have imagined standing here, pledging my life and love to not one, but three men.

The Edin of six months ago was lost, empty, clinging to a life that felt increasingly hollow. Now, as I gazed into the eyes of my men, I felt more whole than I ever thought possible.

"Edin," the celebrant said, her eyes finding mine. "Do you have words for your beloveds?"

I took a deep breath, my heart pounding. We'd decided to speak our own vows, and I'd agonised over mine for weeks. How could mere words capture the depth of what I felt for these men?

"I once felt empty," I said, my voice catching. "A void inside me that nothing could fill. But now..." I squeezed their hands, drawing strength from their touch. "Now I am whole. You three are my heart, my soul, my home."

Tears pricked at my eyes. Finlay's freckled cheeks flushed pink while Knox's cocky grin melted into a warm, genuine smile. A small, sincere smile tugged at the corner of Rhydian's lips, transforming his normally guarded features.

"Rhydian, your strength and protection make me feel safer than I've ever been. Knox, your joy and passion remind me to embrace every moment. Finlay, your wisdom and gentleness soothe my restless spirit."

As I spoke, the soulbond surged through my veins

like molten gold. It was more than just the fiery crackle of my own magic, more than the cool shadows or earthy strength or bright curiosity of my bondmates. It was all those things and more, a symphony of power and passion, an unbreakable weave.

I met each of their gazes in turn, overwhelmed by the love I saw reflected there. "Together, you've shown me what it means to be truly loved, truly accepted. I vow to cherish and nurture this bond between us for all our days, to face whatever challenges come our way with courage and faith in our love."

The celebrant nodded to Rhydian and he cleared his throat, suddenly looking uncharacteristically nervous. Knox chuckled at the sight, earning himself a glare.

"I've spent most of my life in the shadows, convinced I was meant to walk alone," he said, his deep voice resonating through the clearing. His green eyes, once so guarded, now shone with open adoration as they met mine. "You've shown me the light." His grip on my hand tightened. "I promise to protect and cherish you, to stand by your side through whatever storms may come. My shadows will never again be a barrier between us, but a shelter to keep you safe."

My heart ached at the raw emotion in Rhydian's voice. It had been so hard for him to accept our bond at first. To hear him speak so openly of his love now... it was more precious than any gift.

Knox spoke next, his usual playful demeanour tempered by the magnitude of the moment. "Our love defies convention," he said, a hint of his trademark grin playing at his lips. "But it's the truest thing I've ever known. I am yours, always. I vow to bring laughter to your days, passion to your nights, and unwavering support for the rest of our lives."

I smiled, shaking my head. Trust Knox to inject a bit of cheekiness into even the most serious of moments.

Finally, it was Finlay's turn. He took a shaky breath, his hazel eyes bright with emotion.

"From the moment we met, I knew you were the missing piece we'd been searching for," he said softly. "You've made us whole in a way I always believed was possible but never dared hope for. I vow to cherish this connection that binds the four of us, to be your partner in both knowledge and love. You've accepted all of us, equally and completely, and I promise to do the same for you – to love every facet of who you are. My heart, my mind, my very soul – they're yours, now and always, as we build this extraordinary life together."

A sniffle from the small gathered crowd drew my gaze. Veronica, wearing a deep blue ceremonial robe, dabbed at her eyes. She was flanked by her own trio of soulmates. The sight of her – my best friend, now mated to three werewolves – was still a bit surreal. But the joy on her face, the way she fit so perfectly between her mates, mirrored my own happiness.

The soulbond pulsed again, stronger this time. It was as if each word, each promise, was weaving another thread into the tapestry of our connection. The feeling was indescribable – warmth and love and belonging all wrapped into one overwhelming sensation.

I knew there would be hard times ahead. We were still in hiding, after all, still looking over our shoulders for the Council's shadows. And there was so much we didn't yet understand — about The Morrigan's goals, about the full extent of what our soulbond could do.

But here and now, hand in hand with my soulmates — my husbands, now — I felt something settle deep in my bones. A rightness, a readiness.

I stared into their eyes — green, blue, hazel — each shining with the same fierce love, the same unshakable commitment. No more hiding, no more doubts. Only this. Only us.

The celebrant smiled, lifting her hands. "By the power of your love and the strength of your vows, I now pronounce you bound in life and in spirit. May your journey together be filled with laughter, your bond deepen with each passing day, and your love for one another know no bounds. Blessed be." She gestured to the cord wrapped around our wrists.

"Blessed be," we echoed, the words thrumming with the power of a spell.

"You may now seal your union with a kiss."

Rhydian moved first, his intense gaze locked onto mine as he leaned in. His lips met mine in a kiss that was both tender and passionate, sending a shiver down my spine. A rare, soft smile on his face claimed his lips when he pulled back.

Blue eyes twinkling with mischief, Knox swept in next. Playfulness and sweetness mingled in his kiss, embodying the exuberance I'd come to cherish. We'd barely parted when Finlay turned my face towards his, cradling my cheek with gentle hands. His reverent kiss spoke volumes, each moment carefully memorised like pages in one of his beloved books. Unshed tears glistened in his hazel eyes as he slowly drew back, overwhelmed by emotion.

Each kiss was unique, a reflection of the man who gave it and the love we shared. Emotion overwhelmed me, choked me, theirs and mine.

This was it — the beginning of our life together, sealed with three perfect kisses.

A whoop sounded from the small gathering of friends who'd come to witness our union. "That's my girl!" Veronica's voice rang out, followed by a playful wolf whistle.

As the ceremony wound down, our small group of friends mingled in the clearing, enjoying an unhealthy amount of wine and beer the local wolves had transported in and some good music. The sound of laughter and conversation filled the air, a welcome change from the tension we'd all been living with for months.

Veronica broke away from her mates and made a beeline for me, wrapping me in a fierce hug.

"I'm so happy for you," she whispered, squeezing me tight.

I hugged her back just as fiercely. "Thanks. I still can't believe this is real sometimes."

She pulled back, grinning. "Well, believe it, because you're stuck with those three hunks now."

I laughed, shaking my head. "Like you're one to talk. How are things with your wolf pack?"

She glanced back at her mates with a look I recognised all too well. Intense, all-consuming love.

"Honestly? It's amazing. I never thought I'd say this,

but being kidnapped by the Council was the best thing that ever happened to me."

I snorted. It helped that she could heal herself. I would not have fared as well if not for Rhydian.

Speak of the devil... He walked away from our group, moving slowly until he reached the tree line. A flicker of confusion passed through me, but I brushed it off. Rhydian had always needed his space sometimes. It was probably just overwhelming for him, being around so many people.

"So," Veronica said, lowering her voice conspiratorially. She eyed me with a mischievous glint in her eye that I knew all too well. "Have you noticed any of the... side perks of the soulbond yet?"

I frowned, confused. "What do you mean?"

Her grin widened. "Oh, you know. The fun stuff. Like this..."

She closed her eyes for a moment, a look of concentration on her face. Suddenly, all three of her mates turned towards us, their expressions a mix of amusement, frustration, and unmistakable lust.

I burst out laughing. "What did you do?"

"Just sent them a little... mental image," Veronica said, waggling her eyebrows. "Try it. Tap into the power of your bond. Think of something really steamy and direct it at your boys."

Still giggling, I closed my eyes, conjuring up a particularly spicy memory from a few nights ago. I focused on the feeling of the bond, imagining pushing the thought through it like I was sending a text message.

When I opened my eyes, I caught Knox and Finlay

stumbling, their drinks spilling as they shared a look of confusion. Then their gazes locked onto me, and I couldn't help but smirk.

"Oh my god," I whispered to Veronica. "It actually worked!"

We dissolved into laughter as Knox and Finlay started making their way towards us, their eyes dark with desire.

"Edin!" A familiar voice called out before they could reach me.

Hamish joined us, a tentative smile on his face. He pulled me into his arms, wrapping me up in a fierce hug. Knox and Finlay stopped in their tracks, exchanging a look before stepping back to give us space. And I was glad that they did. It had been years since my brother and I had gotten on, even longer since we'd felt a want to hug the other.

Now I clung to him, unashamedly. I'd missed him. I breathed in his familiar scent – old books and the faint tang of magical components.

"I'm so happy you came," I said, my voice catching.

"Wouldn't miss my little sister's big day." He released me, stepping but with a grimace. "Even if it is the strangest wedding I've ever seen."

I laughed. "Well, nothing about my life is exactly normal these days."

"True enough." Hamish's lips quirked in a small smile. "I'm proud of you, Edin, You've faced things I never imagined, and you've come out stronger for it. Mum and Dad would be proud too."

A sob caught in my throat at the mention of our parents. "You think so?"

"I know so. You've found love, real love. That's all they ever wanted for us."

I nodded, unable to speak past the lump in my throat. Instead, I hugged him again, pouring all my gratitude and love into the embrace.

Knox and Finlay approached, their eyes still smouldering from the mental image I'd sent. They stopped at my side, each of them wrapping an arm around my waist. They nodded politely to Hamish, who eyed them with a mix of curiosity and brotherly protectiveness.

"It's nice to finally meet you in person, Hamish," Finlay said. "Though I suppose our first encounter was... rather unconventional."

My cheeks burned at the unnecessary reminder.

Hamish coughed, clearly uncomfortable. "Yes, well, let's not revisit that particular memory, shall we?"

Veronica chuckled. "I don't know, I think it could be fun to watch you all squirm."

"Can't. Other plans," Knox muttered, his voice gruff. "As much as we'd love to chat, we were hoping to borrow our lovely bride for a moment."

The way his voice dipped left little doubt about their intentions. Hamish's eyebrows shot up, while Veronica's grin widened.

"Don't do anything I wouldn't do." She winked.

I laughed. "Pretty sure that leaves everything on the table."

Getting soulbound to three wolves had turned her into quite the exhibitionist.

As Knox and Finlay led me away, I glanced back to see Hamish shaking his head, a bemused expression on his face.

We made our way to a quieter corner of the clearing, away from the main group. Rhydian was still nowhere to be seen, but before I could dwell on it, Finlay's hand cupped my cheek, turning my face towards his.

"That was quite the mental image you sent us, Mrs MacKenzie," he said, his eyes dark with desire.

They'd all chosen to take my name for the sake of simplicity.

I smirked. "Just a little preview of the honeymoon."

Knox's arm snaked around my waist, pulling me flush against him. "Why wait?" he breathed against my ear, sending a shiver down my spine.

I melted into their embrace, overwhelmed by the love and desire flowing through our bond. As our lips met in a kiss, I knew down to my bones that no matter what tomorrow held, I — we — would never be empty again.

EPILOGUE 2

RHYDIAN

The laughter and music from the celebration faded as I slipped deeper into the woods. Shadows clung to me, my body instinctively merging with the darkness gathering between the trees. The scent of ritual herbs still clung to my clothes, mingling with the earthy aroma of the forest floor.

I absentmindedly twisted my new ring around my finger, the weight of it still foreign. My vows that still rang in my ears, almost drowning out the whisper of intuition that had drawn me away from the others.

I promise to protect and cherish you, to stand by your side through whatever storms may come.

I'd meant every word. But barely an hour had passed, and already that promise was being put to the test.

Something was wrong. I could feel it in my bones, in the way the shadows seemed to writhe with unease around me. Years of honed instinct screamed danger, and I'd learned long ago to trust those instincts.

As I moved silently through the underbrush, I cursed myself. For a moment, just a moment, I'd let myself believe we could have this. That we could carve out a slice of happiness in this world that seemed determined to tear us apart.

I should have known better.

A twig snapped somewhere to my left, and I froze. The forest had gone unnaturally still, the birdsong silenced. I reached out with my senses, feeling the ebb and flow of the shadows around me. There — a flicker of movement, too controlled to be an animal.

I melted into the nearest patch of darkness, becoming one with the shadows as I crept closer to the source of the disturbance. Voices drifted towards me, low and urgent.

"...sure this is the place?"

"Positive. The tracking spell led us right to this area."

"Then where are they? I don't see any signs of a ceremony or—"

"Quiet," a third voice hissed. "Remember your training. They could be anywhere."

My blood ran cold as I recognised the clipped, precise tones of Witches Council assassins. How had they found us? We'd been so careful, layering protection spells and misdirection charms around our safe house and the ceremony site.

I inched closer, my heart pounding. Through a gap in the foliage, I could make out five figures dressed in the nondescript dark clothing favoured by Council operatives. They moved with the fluid grace of trained killers, spreading out in a search pattern.

Fury rose within me. How dare they? How dare they try to shatter this one perfect day?

Before I could stop myself, a low growl rumbled from my chest. The nearest assassin whirled, eyes wide.

"He's here!" she shouted, magic flaring to life around her hands.

So much for the element of surprise.

I burst from the shadows, my own power surging through me. Tendrils of darkness lashed out, wrapping around the woman's ankles and yanking her off her feet. She hit the ground hard as I dove for cover behind a massive oak.

Spells exploded around me, sizzling against tree bark and scorching the earth. I reached deep into the well of my magic, feeling it respond eagerly to my call. The shadows of the forest deepened, writhing and coiling like living things.

"Come out and face us, shadow-walker!" one of the assassins called. "The Council sends its regards!"

I almost laughed. As if I'd fall for such an obvious taunt.

Instead, I sent my awareness spiralling outward, mapping the positions of each attacker through the shadows they cast. Five of them, spread out in a rough semicircle. Two to my left, one directly ahead, two more circling to flank me on the right.

I took a deep breath, centering myself. Then I moved.

Shadows enveloped me as I stepped between worlds, emerging behind the assassin on the far left. Before he could react, I slammed the heel of my hand into the base of his skull. He crumpled without a sound.

One down.

A blast of searing heat grazed my shoulder as I dove and rolled. The female assassin I'd downed earlier was back on her feet, her hands wreathed in flames.

"You can't hide forever!" she snarled, hurling another fireball in my direction.

I smirked, even as I ducked behind a fallen log. "Watch me."

The shadows responded to my will, stretching and warping unnaturally. Suddenly, the clearing was filled with dozens of me — shadow clones darting between the trees, drawing fire and sowing confusion.

As the assassins wasted precious magic trying to hit my decoys, I struck again. This time I targeted the one I'd pegged as their leader, a tall man with a shock of silver hair. He was good — I had to give him that. Even as I materialised behind him, he was already spinning to face me, a wickedly curved dagger in his hand.

Our blades clashed, driving me back a step before I could brace myself. He was strong, but I was faster.

I feinted left, then dropped low, sweeping his legs out from under him. As he fell, I brought the pommel of my dagger down hard on his temple. His eyes rolled back and he went limp.

Two down. Three to go.

A scream of rage tore through the air. The fire-witch had spotted me. She abandoned all pretence of stealth and charged forward. Flames roared to life around her, so hot they scorched the air, making it difficult to breathe.

For a heartbeat, all I could see was Edin. Edin, with her fiery hair and amber eyes that burned with passion. Edin, who had taught me that fire could warm as well as destroy.

The moment of distraction nearly cost me everything.

I barely managed to step into the shadows in time. The assassin's attack slammed into empty air while I reappeared behind her. I reached around her, slicing her skin with my dagger, severing her jugular. With a choked sound of pain, she crumpled to the ground, unmoving.

I didn't have time to catch my breath. The last two assassins were on me in an instant, working in tandem with the fluid grace of long-time partners. One wielded twin short swords that sang through the air. The other's hands crackled with arcs of lightning, the hairs on my arms standing on end from the charge in the air.

I gave ground, letting the shadows wrap around me like armour as I parried and dodged. My mind raced, searching for an opening, a weakness I could exploit.

There — the swordsman favoured his left side ever so slightly. And the lightning-witch's attacks left her open for a split second after each strike.

I bided my time, letting them think they had me on the defensive. Then, in the space between one heartbeat and the next, I sprang into action.

I dropped into a low crouch, the swordsman's blade whistling over my head close enough to clip a few strands of hair. As he overextended, I surged upward, driving my shoulder into his sternum. The breath whooshed out of him and he staggered back.

Before his partner could capitalise on my momentary vulnerability, I once again called on every ounce of my power. Shadows exploded outward from me in a dizzying vortex. They cocooned around the lightning-witch, muffling her cry of alarm as they dragged her into the spaces between worlds.

I held her there for one heartbeat, two, three... just long enough for the darkness and disorientation to render her unconscious. Then I released my hold, letting her limp form tumble back into our reality.

The swordsman had regained his footing, eyes wide with a mixture of fear and awe. "What *are* you?" he gasped.

I advanced on him, my voice low and deadly calm. "I am the thing that lurks in dark corners. I am the chill that runs down your spine when you think you're alone. I am vengeance."

His swords clattered to the ground as he raised his hands in surrender. "Please," he begged. "We were just following orders. We didn't—"

My fist connected with his jaw, cutting off whatever excuses he'd been about to spout. As he crumpled, I grabbed a fistful of his shirt, hauling him up to eye level.

"Listen closely," I growled. "When you wake up, you're going to deliver a message to your masters. Tell them that we won't be found so easily next time. Tell them that if they come for my family again, there won't be enough left of them to fill a thimble. Do you understand?"

He nodded frantically, terror plain on his face. I released him, letting him fall in an ungraceful heap.

As I secured the last of the assassins, a slow clap echoed through the clearing. I scowled as Cian emerged from the shadows, a smirk playing on his lips.

Of course, the fucker would hide while I dealt with his minions.

"Impressive work, shadow-walker. You've certainly improved since our last encounter."

"Sending your lackeys to do your dirty work now, Cian?" I growled, shadows coiling around my fists. "Afraid to face me yourself?"

His jaw clenched, a flicker of anger in his eyes. Then he composed himself, a nasty grin spreading across his face. "You know, your little fire witch screamed so prettily when we had her. Does she have nightmares about me?"

Red clouded my vision. With a roar, I lunged at him, shadows exploding outward. Cian dodged, but not fast enough. My fist connected with his jaw, sending him sprawling.

He laughed, spitting blood. "There's the monster I remember."

We clashed in a fury of fists and magic.

His magic crackled through the air, aiming for my weak spots. I countered each strike, my shadows dancing around us. Cian's eyes widened as I anticipated his every move.His moves were predictable, his ego having dulled his edge over the years. He relied on the same dirty tricks — a hidden blade here, a whispered curse there.

I'd seen it all before.

He'd grown complacent, believing his own hype, while I'd honed my skills every single day.

I'd trained every day until exhaustion won in preparation for a day just like this one. If they thought they'd take my family unaware again, they needed to think again.

I fainted left, then swept his legs out from under him. As he fell, I pounced, pinning him to the ground. My shadows wrapped around his throat, choking off his taunts.

"You lose," I snarled.

Fear flickered in his eyes, replaced quickly by defiance. 'Kill me then," he wheezed. "Prove me right."

I leaned in close, savouring the moment. "Oh no. Death's too good for you."

My shadows engulfed him, dragging him into the space between worlds. When we emerged, heat blasted my face. Lava bubbled and hissed around us.

His eyes widened as he took in the volcanic landscape. "You wouldn't dare—"

I grinned, all teeth and savage satisfaction. "Enjoy your new home, Cian. I hear Bouvet Island is lovely this time of year."

We stood on a narrow ledge inside the volcano's crater, heat shimmering the air around us. He stumbled, nearly tumbling into the molten inferno below. My hand shot out, grabbing his shirt and yanking him back from the edge.

"Careful now. Wouldn't want you to fall just yet."

His curses echoed off the volcanic walls as my shadows whisked me away, back to the forest.

As I returned to securing the other assassins, a dark chuckle escaped me. Let him rot in paradise, as far from Scotland — and Edin — as possible. It was almost poetic.

A twinge of doubt crept in. Maybe leaving him alive wasn't the smartest move. Edin had made me promise to kill less, but she might regret that if Cian ever got his hands on her again. This would only delay him as long as it took to climb out of that volcano.

I shook off the thought. What's done was done. I'd deal with him again if I had to. For now, I had a family to protect.

As the rush of battle faded, exhaustion hit me like a physical blow. I surveyed the unconscious forms of the assassins, my mind already racing ahead to what needed to be done next.

We'd stayed too long. I'd known it for weeks, but I hadn't wanted to be the one to shatter that happiness.

But now I had no choice.

The others wouldn't like it. We'd put down roots here, carved out a semblance of normalcy with the local wolf pack despite the constant threat hanging over our heads. Edin had her research, Knox had found work at a local wildlife sanctuary, and Finlay had practically taken up residence in the nearby library.

But none of that mattered if we were dead.

As I began the process of securing the assassins —

binding their magic and transporting each one thousands of miles away — I weighed our options.

We could find another safe house in Scotland, but the risk of discovery would only increase. The Council clearly had some way of tracking us, even through our wards and protections.

No, we needed to go further. Somewhere entirely new, where the Council's reach was limited.

The beginnings of a plan began to take shape in my mind. I had contacts — old debts I could call in, favours I could leverage. It would take some doing, but I could get us out of the country. Somewhere warm, maybe. Edin would like that — she was always complaining about the damp Scottish weather.

My gaze drifted back towards the celebration, though the trees blocked it from view. How was I going to tell them? How could I ask them to uproot their lives yet again, to leave behind everything they'd built here?

But even as doubt gnawed at me, I felt the warm pulse of our bond. Four hearts beating as one, four souls inexorably intertwined.

As I made my way back through the woods, I rehearsed what I'd say in my head. We'd celebrate tonight — they deserved that much. But come morning, we'd need to be ready to run.

The sounds of laughter and music grew louder as I approached the clearing. I paused at the edge of the trees, drinking in the sight of my family lost in the joy of the moment.

Edin threw her head back, laughing at something Knox had said. Finlay's arm was draped around her waist, a soft smile on his face as he watched them. They looked so happy, so carefree.

For a moment, just a moment, I let myself imagine a world where we could stay like this forever. Where we didn't have to constantly look over our shoulders, always one step ahead of those who would tear us apart.

But that world didn't exist. Not yet, anyway.

I squared my shoulders and stepped out of the shadows. Time to be the bearer of bad news once again.

But as Edin's eyes found mine, lighting up with a warmth that never failed to take my breath away, a flicker of hope sprang to life in my chest.

I hope you enjoyed Bound By The Goddess.
If you're like me, the end is never enough, subscribe to my newsletter and grab a bonus epilogue fro Knox's POV. I promise there's more steamy times ahead.

You've probably guessed The Morrigan's next victim: Veronica.

Marked By The Goddess will release in the first quarter of 2025. I'm not setting a date on it until it's written.

If you'd like to preorder the ebook directly from me and get early access, you can do so on my website until March 2025.

Otherwise, follow me on Amazon to be notified when the preorder or paperback book goes live.

ABOUT SELINA

Selina Bevan is a British paranormal romance author who writes delicious heroes and captivating worlds, delving deep into the magic and love, with witches, deities, and a spectrum of supernatural beings finding their soulmates in the most unexpected places.

She is a chai tea addict who loves a good gig and finding new alt-rock music when mindlessly scrolling Instagram at night.

Selina writes MF and RH/Why Choose romances with strong-willed but flawed British heroines.

Milton Keynes UK
Ingram Content Group UK Ltd.
UKHW031305251024
450245UK00004B/252